I0822807

RICK S. GLOWAKI

DARSHAN and the DECEASED

Jodi K Costa LLC
Tampa, Florida

Shine Press
4522 W Village Dr. #1294
Tampa, FL 33624
Shine Press is an imprint of Jodi K Costa, LLC

Cover Artist: Julia Alexander

Hardcover ISBN: 979-8-9909367-5-1

Manufactured in the United States of America
For permission requests, please contact the publisher at Shine-Press.com

TIBET
MAY, 1982

As soon as Ryder Nowacki heard the taxi's plaintiff cry off in the distance he just knew his Uncle William would have something to say about it. Ryder was still taken aback when his uncle's response immediately came.

"Taxi horns, specifically Paris taxi horns." Ryder's Uncle William James stated as the four men continued their trek. "That's what I'm hearing."

"William," explained Nick , "we're in Asia, not even close to France."

"Ah, but the sounds of the Tibetan taxi and the Parisian taxi of the 1920's are very similar!" William countered.

"And how would you even know that? Or prove that?" Nick Brown asked as the four continued on foot as dust and Yak dung kicked up from their boots in the evening air. They had been hiking the previous three hours after their taxi, lorry, or bus (they heard it referred to as all three) broke down amid hissing steam and billowing smoke from the engine, and had not seen another person yet.

"George Gershwin came to Paris specifically to hunt for Parisian taxi horns for the Broadway show he was working on, 'An American in Paris'." William explained while ignoring any of the comments the other men were saying both under and over their breath. This went on for almost another kilometer.

Nick, along with Dave Highland, had known William since their college days in the Midwest. The three men were all forty-two years old. This was a reunion of sorts for the three as they stared middle age in the face.

Dave went into the financial world of the Chicago Mercantile Exchange where he made very good money trading lumber and hog futures. Nick started in job recruiting but then pivoted over to writing proposals for local governments that were looking for grants and big federal contracts. Neither man wanted for money.

William had been a mountain guide the world over ever since he left the Peace Corps after college graduation. He made decent money as a guide but for him the important caveat was the adventures and the lands he got to experience. It was on those quiet nights with no radio or television to distract him that he read voraciously. He read not only his own books but any books his clients would bring along as well. William knew a lot of things about a lot of things, and he knew he knew a lot of things about a lot of things and sometimes that got annoying. Also, it got kind of annoying how good looking and tall William was for any of the men around him seeing as the women only seemed to have eyes for him.

When this latest trip came together he thought of his sixteen year old nephew, Ryder. His sister's boy had been having a tough time of it since the father walked out on the family. At least that's what it seemed the last time he had visited his sister and Ryder a couple of years ago. William explained to his sister how good he thought a trek like this would be for the boy. Fresh air, strenuous hiking, and the company of fine grown men to emulate. His sister was all for it, it was Ryder who needed convincing, though not because he was shy or out of shape but because three months previously he had fallen deeply in love.

"Town!" Dave shouted and pointed to the horizon.

"Kangding!" William said feeling suddenly very pleased.

"Kangding," Nick said, putting his hand up to his ear like it was a telephone, "kangding. It's for you Ryder!" Ryder laughed and then kept the smile on his face as it always felt good when he was included by any of the three men. They were such old and close friends, and also almost three decades older than he was, that it was easy for Ryder to feel out of place and a bit alone with them.

"Kangding is a centuries old hub-town for the tea routes to Lhasa." William explained. William always seemed to explain. As the four walked further the town appeared to grow taller and William continued to teach how the tea grown across Yunnan and Sichuan would converge there at Kangding and then proceed by armed caravan to Batang, Chamdo, and at last Lhasa.

"Of course it does, William, of course it does." Nick said, cutting him off. "I just want to know if we're going to sleep on a real bed or in a tent."

"I'll ask around and we'll look around." William said while cinching up his rucksack as he was apt to do when he wanted to seem even more in charge. It was one of the mannerisms Ryder noticed from his uncle that he found himself starting to do as well.

An hour later they were in the town. Ryder looked to his left and there was a pig hung by its ankles from a tree while a man drew a knife down its belly and yards of blue intestines slithered over his arm. Ryder looked away to his right side and saw a woman move through a rare shaft of sunlight with a baby slung on her front. Prayer flags flapped everywhere in the breeze that never seemed to stop. William was talking to a thin young man who looked just slightly older than Ryder.

"You can call me Paul. I run a Christian guest house just down the road. There." Paul said and jutted his finger out to a two story building that was covered in layers of mountain dust, as all the old buildings in that town were.

Paul was shorter than the three men but taller than Ryder and dark skinned. "From India?" William guessed and Paul nodded.

Paul, Dave, Nick, and Ryder were all impressed with William's guess, as William was hoping they would be when he said it.

"I was born in Sri Lanka but then I was schooled in the Indian Himalayas." Paul said and then began to lead the four to his building. "Are you looking for lodging only for tonight?"

"Yes, just tonight." William answered. "Your English is impeccable."

"I also speak Sinhalese, Hindi, Chinese, and Tibetan."

"Wow, I just speak English and American." Nick said, trying to make everyone laugh. Only Ryder obliged.

William ignored his old college buddy's attempt at humor and spoke again to Paul, "So you're a missionary of sorts?"

"No," Paul corrected him, "not a missionary, but my faith informs everything that I do here."

When they were out of Paul's earshot William whispered to his friends, "He's a missionary."

The four were very appreciative of the beds that Paul provided along with the fact that he didn't try to evangelize them and the three older men were asleep and snoring within a few minutes after they laid down. Ryder looked out of the window that his bed was near and stared at the sky, and the countless array of stars and thought. He had seen so many amazing vistas, and valleys, and peaks, and people so far during the journey. Yet all Ryder thought about was her.

***

Paul helped secure transportation (some would call it a taxi, others a lorry, still others would say it's a bus) for the seven hour drive to the pass of Zheduo at nearly 16,500 feet. The thin air made everyone sleepy but as of yet only William and Dave were asleep as the vehicle bumped and trundled along the dusty highway towards the still unseen great mountain. Both men were in the front of the vehicle while Nick and Ryder were in the last row of seats.

As they approached a tunnel, a deeper than normal pothole catapulted the vehicle high into the air and then it landed with a set of bumps which promptly woke up William but not Dave. William was at first nonplussed but then seeing the tunnel said, "A tunnel! C.M. Forster once said -"

"Who?" Nick asked with his arms folded and still looking out of the window at the passing landscape. There were smooth plains and a slight elevation as far as his eyes could currently see. This part of the journey could become annoyingly tedious. Long hours through a barren and brown land.

William ignored or maybe did not hear Nick ask that question and went right on with his dissertation, "that tunnels are our gates to the glorious and unknown. Through them we pass out into adventure and sunshine."

Nick, who was sitting next to Ryder, thought about that sentence and leaned in close to Ryder and whispered, "I hate to admit it, but your uncle is right about that tunnel stuff. That's a pretty cool quote." Nick then sat back in his seat.

Ryder smiled and nodded at Nick.

Nick then leaned in and stressed to Ryder, "But whatever you do do not tell him I said that!"

Ryder held out his hand and Nick shook it and then Ryder smiled brightly and said, "It's a deal!"

More prayer flags whipping in the wind. Stone cairns. Occasionally a person was seen walking while wrapped up in what looked like billowing sheets to ward off the elements. Wind, always wind, and dust. Closer, they proceeded, closer still to the mountain that they had yet to see. Bugs continued to get smashed loudly by the thousands against the windshield and the driver would laugh every time it happened.

As they got higher elevations, bits of snow would fly past the windows at ridiculous speeds and they joined the bugs to form a black and white kaleidoscope. Beyond their vehicle to the west was a wide river valley, dry and lunar, through which ran a river of white ice and blue water. It was getting noticeably colder. Ryder nudged Nick and pointed to a group of dung tailed yaks walking aimlessly in a farmer's field near their road. Also in the field lay lines of snow, thawed from the summits of the plough lines but holding white in the trenches.

With all there was to see the time was going by quickly for Ryder. As he stared at nothing in particular and the whole landscape became a blur out of his window, his mind went back to the United States and the girl he fell madly in love with just three months previously. The girl that was much too beautiful and brilliant for him and yet she loved him, or at least she declared she did in both letters and to his face.

A bump in the road woke Dave from a nap and after he looked around to gain his bearings he saw Ryder looking back at him. Dave scrunched up his face in wonder and asked the teenager, "Don't you have to do a paper on Albert Einstein for school?"

"Yes, for Science class. But I also have to do one for English class on -"

Dave continued, "Albert Einstein was a genius."

Ryder agreed with him and said, "Yes he was."

"But his brother Frank was a monster." Dave then closed his eyes while it took Ryder a moment to get the joke.

Smiling now, Ryder unzipped the pocket that held his wallet and after much grabbing was able to pull it out from his seated position. He opened it and flipped through the plastic picture section and there she was in her resplendent glory and pulchritude (his uncle taught him that fancy word for beauty!). Her smile radiating warmth and love while her eyes seemed to call out his name in a loving request.

"Pretty girl." Nick said which jolted Ryder out of his blissful repose.

Ryder wasn't sure what to say to that. To say 'thank you' would imply he had a hand in her looks and genetics. To say 'I know' would be smug and boastful. So instead Ryder replied honestly, "She is. Inside and out."

Nick smiled. He knew. Nick was still in love with his wife of fourteen years. When it really happened it was rare and wonderful. When it went off the rails and askew, it was Dave's life.

Nick did not want to tell Ryder but Dave was in the process of getting separated from his wife of seventeen years. Almost two decades and two sons later

Dave's marriage was going off the rails and totally askew. Dave needed this trip. He needed a distraction. That's how he was able to talk Nick into going with him after William first asked.

"Treat her right, kid." Nick said to Ryder while still looking at her two pictures that were open for him to see. "Never let her doubt how much you feel."

Ryder quickly affirmed, "She'll never doubt!"

"Want to see my two girls?" Nick asked and Ryder looked a bit confused so Nick then elaborated, "My wife and daughter."

Ryder smiled, nodded and then looked at a picture of Nick and his wife on their wedding day and then of another one of Nick's three year old adorable daughter.

"They're gorgeous! You are very lucky!"

"If I believed in luck I'd agree with you. I think I'm more blessed. Blessed to have Susan as my wife and Valerie as my little girl."

Ryder sat quietly and thought about what Nick just said. He never really thought about the difference between being lucky and being blessed. He never thought either that there might be no such thing as luck as Nick stated.

Nick leaned down and took a closer look at the pictures of Ryder's girlfriend and said to him, "She's much too pretty for you." He then turned away, refolded his arms, and closed his eyes.

Ryder smiled and then dug down and got his rucksack from underneath the seat in front of him and positioned it so it would act as a pillow against the window. He folded his arms against the cold and closed his eyes just for a minute.

Another pothole jolted all the passengers and Dave yelled out to William, "Quite a road you picked for us!"

"Be happy we're even in a vehicle, Dave!" William shot back. "Until 1950 Tibet was a country without wheels."

"What does that even mean?" Dave asked as Nick and Ryder also wondered the same thing.

"Travel in Tibet by air, car, or cart was forbidden." William answered and waited for the next obvious question.

Nick provided it. "Why?"

"For fear of scarring the earth and releasing evil spirits." William answered and was pleased with himself for providing yet another interesting, he hoped, fact about this exotic country.

Ryder again folded his arms against the cold and decided to once more close his eyes for just a minute.

***

Ryder's minute of having his eyes closed lasted nearly two hours. His wavy, light brown hair was half matted down and half sticking up in three different directions. When he first opened his eyes he had no idea that he was traveling through Tibet, he momentarily thought he was on a school bus or something along those lines.

"Ah, look who is back amongst the living!" William said theatrically upon seeing that Ryder was now awake. "We were just talking about the mountain we're going to."

"Oh." That was all Ryder could manage to say as he was still getting his bearings from that unexpected nap, which coupled with the jet lag and the thirteen hour difference in times between the United States and Tibet left the teenager less than eloquent. Still, he kept a positive disposition and was not one to complain. He rolled with the punches that life threw at him. And now that he was deeply in love with the girl of his dreams, Ryder knew he could handle almost anything as long as they were together.

"Do you have any questions about the trek or the mountain itself?" William asked while offering Ryder a banana to eat.

“Ryder shook his head and said, “No thank you, Uncle.” and looked out of his window in the direction he thought the mountain would be. “We still can’t see it?”

“Soon, my boy, not yet.” Uncle William answered his nephew. “When we do, it’ll all be worth it!”

“Oh,” Ryder said, suddenly remembering a question he had now that his brain was becoming more clear, “yeah, what is our mountain we’re climbing called again?” Nick and Dave both laughed.

His Uncle William patiently answered his nephew, “Minya Konka. It’s a sacred mountain known as the white snow peak of the kingdom of Minyak. It’s just under 25,000 feet tall. And it rises in easterly isolation as the last great upsurge of the Central Asian ranges.”

“Who talks like this?” Nick asked in reference to Williams’ esoteric eloquence.

Dave pointed his thumb at William and replied, “That clown.” Old friends can say such things to each other. It is almost expected.

William did what he often would do upon hearing one of his friend’s put downs, he ignored it. “But we’re not climbing it.”

“Oh yes, circumnavigate it?” Ryder asked his uncle.

“Close, my boy, circumambulate, but we’re not quite doing that either. What we’re going to do is -”

“Town!” Excitedly said Karim, their driver, as they hurtled down that dusty and bumpy road. It was the first words Ryder had heard him say. Most of the time he was just singing Tibeto-pop songs in a gleaned voice while the landscape streamed past. He wore a black leather jacket with a Led Zeppelin Swan Song escutcheon embroidered on its sleeve.

Karim was generous in his description of that place being a town, it was anything but. It was five buildings that all belonged to the same man, Dorje. The men knew this all belonged to Dorje because as soon as they arrived a man sauntered down a nearby hill just as dusk was setting and casually stated, "I am Dorje, all this is mine, you may sleep in tents in my yard for five yuan." He paused for effect and then said, "Each."

Dave, Nick, and Ryder all looked to William to see if this was an agreeable arrangement. William looked into the sky and pondered broadly and then smiled at Dorje and finally answered, "Yes!"

Dorje smiled back, nodded his head and while clasping his hands walked away into the main building.

"That's less than a dollar a piece." William explained with a gleeful look to the other three. "And besides, where else are we going to go?"

Once the people and the rucksacks were unpacked, Karim disappeared behind a tree, relieved himself, and then sped off in the direction that they came without even a goodbye. "Not one for sentiment I reckon." William surmised while watching the dust clouds rise behind Karim's wheels.

Dorje's family compound was located under a swatch of red rock at 13,000 feet above sea level. Had a high range of mountains not blocked its appearance, Dorje's land faced east and right towards Minya Konka.

The men heard children's laughter coming from inside the wide-walled and heavy tiled building that Dorje had disappeared into. It was obvious the sturdy buildings had seen many a winter and were built to see many more. The wooden shutters had been intricately carved and colored with reds, golds, and blues. Every now and then a bright faced Tibetan child would stick its head out of the windows that those shutters covered. Decorative lines of orange rock had been built into the walls like strata.

Dorje invited the four Americans into his house for dinner and there they met his six children, his wife, his two sister in laws, both of their husbands, and all of their children. Despite the language barrier the men were able to be animated and made the children laugh often. Here Dave really came into his own and performed various juggling routines as well as many pratfalls. The kids ate his antics up. Ryder felt like it was the first time on this adventure that Dave looked truly happy.

Nick found a cherubic three year old daughter of one of the relatives of Dorje and played with her and then after she fell asleep in his arms he continued to hold her. Nick found out from her mother that her daughter he was holding was named Dolma, which meant 'savioress' or 'liberator'. "Well she sure liberated my heart." Nick said softly to no one in particular as he gazed down on the sleeping child he was gently rocking in his arms. This was the first time on the trip that Nick seemed sad or at least pensive. William, being robbed of his main advantage - ostentatious speech - due to the language barrier, was mostly reserved and silent. William took out his camera and methodically attached a small lens and began to take pictures of the people, the surroundings, and especially of Nick sitting with the three year old daughter of the relative of the owner.

And then there was the call to sit at the long wooden tables for the feast. Ryder just ate the rice and the potatoes and not the meat which he could not quite identify. The three older men ate sumptuously and then they all retired to the yard where they climbed into their tent and slept under a shovel full of stars while the moon illuminated the tops of distant mountains and bounced the lights every which way.

As Ryder lay there next to the three snoring men he pondered on when he should begin writing his essay for school. He knew he was not going to start it that night, but sometime soon he would have to. That was the condition for his high school letting him skip the final two weeks of the year, he had to document at length his trip and the cultures and geography he experienced. He was also required to take his final exams a couple of weeks before his other classmates and though he thought he passed them, he felt he did barely. Ryder tried to organize his thoughts for how he would start to write his paper, but all he could think about instead was the last evening he spent with his true love and the enraptured and euphoric feelings she aroused in him.

She had given him a platinum spoon that night, wrapped up beautifully in an ornate little rectangular box and topped with a bow she had made herself. When he eagerly unwrapped it and saw what it was Ryder was perplexed. She then told a parable, she was always telling parables and Ryder found them fascinating and such a different way to communicate her points. In this parable, a woman had many spoons, but only one platinum spoon, and it was her favorite and so cherished. She kept it safe and secure and didn't let anything bad happen to it but she still used it everyday. "That is how I think of you, Ryder, you're my platinum spoon."

It made Ryder smile to remember that parable, and that night, and her. There was something so uplifting in his spirit when he thought about her. Though never an insecure young man, there was a confidence her love gave Ryder. He felt like people looked at him differently when someone so beautiful as her was by his side. Ryder felt taller around her, and more important. He thought others, especially his school mates, must think highly of him for being her beau. To ever lose her…he could not even think about it. But then his mind began to go to a place where feasibly she did leave him, possibly for another man. Ryder could not shake those terrible thoughts from his head. The thoughts that in his absence she had grown tired of waiting for him and began to date another. Sleep did not come easy or quickly that night for Ryder.

***

The rest of the journey would all be under their own power. There were no more roads and barely any trails except for foot traffic and yak parades. The golden sun shone above but provided little or no heat, not at their present elevation of 15,000 feet above sea level. As the four hiked further and higher through Tibet their breathing became more labored and ragged. Their steps slowed as fatigue began to take over and they tried to be extra careful. The nice thing about not traveling by vehicle anymore is that their hearing became part of the Tibetan equation.

The men could now hear the flapping of the prayer flags that seemed to pop up in the most remote places of the trail, and usually attached to cairns several feet high and composed of white stones.

Ryder made William's morning when he asked him about the white stones they often saw that made up the cairns. "Why my boy, that's because white stones have a particular force on the Qiang people of Northern Sichuan. They gather up white quartz and marble shards and heap them in these cairns, some of which are vast! I've seen ones dozens of meters in diameter. The cairns mark the landscape's most sacred points."

The talking then stopped again, it was too much work to walk, breath, and talk. So the ears took over again. As they passed near a valley they could faintly hear the water rushing but what stood out the most to their ears were the hollow sound of boulders being rolled by the current on the riverbed. They heard the crunching of their own boots as they followed the bare trace of a path. Huge birds, that not even William could name if he had five guesses, were heard overhead making their various hooting and chirping as they rode the updraft higher into the blue air. They heard their own breathing as they gasped for more oxygen to feed their thinning supply as they went higher.

"Shall we stop here for a bit of lunch?" William asked the group as they approached an unsteady wooden bridge that was swaying over a frigid river. The water was frozen at the river's margins but it was flowing deep and green in the center.

"William, I love you!" Nick said in exhaustion and dropped his rucksack right where he stood. He then plopped down and used the bag for a pillow.

"So I take it that's a 'yes' from Nick?" Dave asked and then also dropped his bag and sort of also collapsed onto the ground. The embankment made for a perfect approximation of a reclining chair for them. The wind was blocked by the surrounding hills and the sun was starting to provide some warmth.

Trail mix and apples with peanut butter smeared on them were devoured by all. Dave sounded like he was actually starting to snore after he finished eating. Ryder made a point to remember this moment for his school paper.

Too soon their respite was over and then they nervously crossed the tottering footbridge, all the while bracing themselves for a polar plunge if any of the wooden planks broke through. None did.

As they continued to trek upwards through the now trackless rising valley that was scrubbed with juniper and vultures wheeling overhead, more and more snow packed the ground. This enabled them to see what creatures crossed there before them. There were many bird tracks as well as fox fonts and scat of numerous unknown living things. Mostly triangular and unclimbed peaks lined the northern sky and the snow became crunchier and louder under foot.

Nick wondered what his little girl and wife were up to at that precise moment. William wondered about the woman he said an impassioned goodbye to in Frankfurt that left him languid for the past few days. Dave wondered where it all went wrong with his matrimonial aspirations. Ryder wondered what the love of his life was up to and if she was still thinking of him.

Four more hours passed. The air got thinner. The crunching under one's boots got louder. Throats got dryer no matter how much water was consumed. Aches in the legs and backs became more numerous.

The trail turned a corner and boom! Suddenly, it was all worth it and all maladies and drawbacks were erased and gone like they were never there. The men stood as one and marveled.

There majestically before them, two miles away, and nearly two miles up, was Minya Konka. "There's a Sanskrit word for when you are gazing at an amazing view, of possibly something holy and much bigger than yourself, it's called Darshan. When I see this mountain that is the word I think of." William admitted.

"Darshan!" Ryder and Dave both said in amazement.

"That's a lot better than the one simple word I thought of to say." Nick replied and then stated the one simple word, "Wow!"

***

Ryder's mother, Joanne Nowacki, was not going to tell her son he could not go on this Tibetan excursion with his Uncle William, but she wished he wouldn't. She was nervous about a myriad of things that could go wrong and in her mind all of them ended up with her son being hurt, or worse. Ever since she divorced her husband she went out of her way to try and protect her only son. He maintained a moderately happy disposition throughout the entire divorce ordeal but she noticed he really only came into his own the past few months. The exact same time frame that her son Ryder met, fell in love, and basically gave his life over to Leanne Rhobbs.

Joanne had nothing personally against Leanne and liked her well enough as a person. Joanne also thought Leanne to be a beautiful looking girl with impeccable manners and was very impressed with her intellect. She just thought her son was losing himself in the love he felt for Leanne.

When she told her son what she thought, Ryder had to admit that his mother might have been correct, but then, what was so wrong, he pondered, with losing oneself in the pursuit of happiness with and for another person? Ryder thought that Christianity had taught him to be selfless and with Leanne he was. All he wanted in life was to see her smile, especially when Leanne smiled at him with those deep brown eyes and glistening white teeth of hers. It took his breath away.

It was this love that he felt for Leanne, or according to his mother, this 'obsession' that led him to wish many times the trip would have been canceled and he wouldn't have to leave the true love of his young life. All through the journey he carried a nagging feeling that he wished he was back home with her. This nagging feeling disappeared, if only briefly, upon rising up that pass and seeing

Minya Konka.

"Ryder, my boy, are you happy now that you came with your old uncle?" William asked his nephew as all four stood motionless at the sight of the majestic mountain and its perfect triangular snow-covered peak.

Ryder nodded and meant every word that he replied to his proud uncle, "I really am now!"

Upon hearing Williams' question and Ryder's reply Nick asked Dave, "Are you happy you came too?"

"I really am now!" Dave replied, sharing Ryder's answer and sentiment and appreciating his friend's concern.

"This view!" Ryder exclaimed, soaking it all in.

"Yes, this view." Uncle William repeated. "You know, two of the first Americans to ever see this view of Minya Konka were a couple of Teddy Roosevelt's sons way back in the early 1920s."

"Early 1920's?" Nick said, "Wait, you don't know the exact year? What's wrong with you William, you're slipping!"

"Yes, what kind of tour guide are you? I want my money back!" Dave added as everyone was now feeling giddy with excitement. The mountain looked so close to them now. Deceptively close. It also appeared to be implausibly easy to ascend from that viewpoint on that wintry and wind blown pass.

"Are we going to climb it tomorrow?" Ryder asked his uncle. To the inexperienced it looked like a simple day long jaunt to the top and Nick and Dave were wondering the same thing. A seasoned mountaineer like William knew how deceiving the ease of the trek would really be.

"We're still a couple of days away from that mountain. Let's keep moving." William commanded as that wind-scoured pass was no place to loiter long. Far below was the river gorge that separated their range from the Konka massif. The four had many miles to go before they slept somewhere down in that valley.

They often slipped and lost their footing as they descended down the shale slopes and their quadriceps and hamstrings burned and ached. At one point Dave lost his footing and began to slide perilously close to the edge of a ravine but Nick was able grab onto his friend's trekking pole and threw himself down on the ground to arrest their fall. The men stopped their impatient descending of going mostly straight down and instead began to employ more switchbacking.

The snow depth varied depending on its exposure to the elements. In many places it was ankle deep and rocks would occasionally show through and reflect the sun's light but in other areas the snow was knee-deep. Here the trek became arduous and the physical exertion to move through it caused the men to sweat profusely despite the sub-freezing temperatures and wind.

By the time they reached the partially frozen stream at the bottom of the valley the men were worn out and needed both rest and sustenance. There was a thick forest of Himalayan oak and pine along with thick bushes of rhododendron and so the men found a small clearing near a shepherd's hut and all laid with their backs against the warm wall of moss covered rocks that faced both the sun and the mountain.

William kept looking at his watch as he knew darkness was not far behind and they needed to get to a suitable camping spot. After twenty minutes that felt like barely twenty seconds the men were fed and on the move again. This time though they still ascended, it was a mostly vertical trek and again through the lush forest.

Two hours later they emerged from the forest at the main river and continued downstream. The men were too tired to speak to each other and though inches apart were alone with their thoughts. Their brains seemed to always think back to what centered them. For Nick, it was his wife and daughter. Dave reexamined his marriage and the mistakes that he knew were his and if it was truly too late fix things. William's thoughts bounced between the practical and the sensual. As he hiked he was scouting out potential places to pitch their tent and he also was thinking back on the last time he went hiking and camping with a Parisian paramour in the Italian alps. Ryder found his mind traveling away from Leanne and more towards what they were finally going to eat and how hopefully soft his sleeping arrangements would be. His energy was sapped and he was famished. No matter how vividly Ryder tried to think back on his last romantic night alone with Leanne before he left for Tibet all he could instead picture was meat, potatoes, and a sleeping bag.

***

The spot William found for their camp that evening was perfectly located for all their needs. Water from a stream was a short walk as was the forest for firewood. There was a nice swath of sunlight that streamed down yet the nearby rock walls blocked most of the wind. As an added bonus it was a generally level little plot of land that was softened by a tuft of soft, green grass.

"Ryder, get us a lot of firewood for the bonfire, and I mean a lot!" William requested while sitting and taking off his boots and then socks. "Dave, you and Nick start putting up the tent. And mind you strap those sides down tight and hammer those poles in deep, we're going to get a goodly amount of wind tonight I'm afraid." William now took off his shirt and pants as well and then wrapped a towel around himself.

Ryder was already in the forest with his hatchet so he did not witness this striping by William.

"Should we even ask?" Nick asked Dave as they both skeptically eyed William as he began to walk away from their camp wearing only a towel.

"Be nice and I'll show you how to make sure your legs feel like they are twenty years old tomorrow." William said while strolling away towards the stream.

After approaching the stream William looked around to make sure he was alone and then laughed at himself for doing that. Really, who else would be in this remote and mostly inhospitable area? He then hung his towel from a nearby branch and then stepped out of his underwear and walked into the frigid stream and sat down so the water covered him up past his belly button. He then looked at his watch and closed his eyes and started to breathe deeply and then slowly let the air out of his lungs.

As they worked on the tent Dave said to Nick, "I kind of want to know but I also don't want to know, you know?"

Nick nodded and continued pounding down the steaks with a hammer for the poles of the tent. After ten minutes Ryder came back from the forest and walked into the clearing holding an impossibly large stack of firewood and branches for kindling.

"Wow!" Dave exclaimed upon seeing the young man carrying so much needed fuel for their bonfire.

"Don't you mean 'darshan'?" Nick asked, correcting him. The three laughed at William's expense.

"Yes you do mean 'darshan'!" William said re-entering the camp site while carrying his clothes and only sporting a towel.

"You took a bath, Uncle William?" Ryder asked, clearly shocked at the thought in such cold conditions.

"Yes, my boy, but not so much for cleanliness. Let me get dressed and I'll gladly explain to you all." The tent was now finished and William disappeared into it to get dressed while Ryder sorted the firewood between small and larger pieces. Nick and Dave sat and rested and watched.

The young man then arranged rocks in a circle and then took the medium sized pieces of wood and made a log cabin type bonfire with them and on top of that placed a large round, fat log. "Does this look good?" Ryder asked the two men who only shrugged their shoulders and then nodded.

"I guess." Dave said.

"My guess is it'll look better with some food cooking on it!" Nick replied just as William came out of the tent fully dressed.

"You two are next." William said to Nick and Dave.

"Next for what?" Dave asked.

"An ice bath." William answered. William thought the two men would ridicule his idea and fight against it and he was not disappointed. Neither man wanted to do such an uncomfortable thing in that climate.

"It's for your own good." William explained. "The muscles you used to get up that pass and then down it are going to be hurting tomorrow, worse than now, unless you take this ice bath. Just ten minutes, that's all you need to help your muscles and soothe their aches and lactic acid."

"How is getting frostbite going to help my leg muscles?" Dave asked and Nick nodded in solidarity.

"I don't know exactly how it all works, but it does work. I've been doing it for years, ever since this man in Switzerland taught me. I've never had sore legs since and I'm just as old as you two!"

After much cajoling the two men finally trudged off to the stream to try William's antidote to leg muscle pain.

"Don't look!" Nick ordered Dave as he took off his underwear.

"You have nothing to see anyway!" Dave said and then also slid out of his underwear. Much yelling and screeching accompanied the submerging of the men in the nearly frosted over stream, but they did it. They made themselves stay seated for ten full minutes and upon getting out they ran in only their towels to the roaring bonfire that Ryder had going at the campsite.

"We hate you, William!" Nick shouted as they shivered and sat as close as they could to the conflagration.

"But you'll love me tomorrow." William replied knowingly with a smile.

"Should I take an ice bath too, Uncle William?" Ryder asked, hoping his uncle would say that he did not need to.

"Sure! Couldn't hurt!" William answered with pep.

"Yes it could! And did!" Nick replied, inching closer still to the warming flames dancing in front of his face.

While Ryder went off to do his ice bath William started to cook their dinner and Nick and Dave got fully dressed again. The two men also arranged the four sleeping bags in the 3 man tent.

"Why a three man tent for four people?" Dave asked William.

"Easier to carry and much warmer at night. I have a bad feeling we're going to freeze tonight." William said, looking up at the clear sky as dusk quickly approached. It was getting darker by the second. "No clouds during the day is nice because the sun can warm you. At night, no clouds means no heat."

"You're not thinking of spooning with me tonight, are you William?" Nick asked sardonically.

"You wish!" William shot back. He then flipped the meat over to cook more and saw that Ryder was coming back to their current base camp. "Hey there nephew, are you still freezing from your ice bath?"

"No William, his lips always turn blue this time of the day." Nick replied and then scooted over so Ryder could sit close to the fire to try to thaw out.

"You have considerably less body fat than those two," William explained with a flip of his thumb towards Nick and Dave, "so the cold probably affected you a lot more. I have a neat little trick to warm yourself up. Actually you two could benefit from this too." William said to Nick and Dave.

"What is it? I'll try anything! I can't get warm!" Dave said while rubbing his arms with his hands. "I'm so cold, I'm not like Nick, William if you do want to spoon please feel free because I can't -"

"Gentleman, or in this case Nick and Dave, do not worry, I will explain." William promised as Dave and Nick looked on eagerly. "There was this eleventh century hermit named Milaprepa and he-"

"Of course there was." Nick said with a sigh and rolling eyes though William paid his friend no heed.

"- and Milaprepa taught a form of tantric yoga called Tumo -"

"Tumo." Dave interrupted William this time. "You writing that down, Ryder? Tumo. There's going to be a test on this later."

Unruffled, William continued, "Practitioners of Tumo were able to generate their own body heat. Even in the high mountains they would only wear one layer of cotton cloth while meditating out here."

"Out here?" Dave asked in amazement, not quite believing it.

"Yes, in fact there is a group of Buddhist Ladakhi cave dwellers that would soak their robes in water and then sit in the winter's wind and steam their cloaks dry using that tantric Tumo power. You know, deep breathing and meditating and so forth. I'll show you. Watch my stomach and then chest." William deeply filled first his stomach and then his chest with a very long and deep breath. Once his chest was fully expanded, he then slowly started to let the air out until there was no more in his lungs. Even then he paused a beat before taking another deep and fulfilling breath.

"See?" William asked. "Each breath in and then out should take about a minute once you really calm down and do it correctly."

"Like this?" Ryder asked and his uncle watched him.

"Very good! But try making the air come out slower and the whole breathing process takes longer." Uncle William instructed.

The other two men began to try this new breathing method. "How many times do we do this before we start getting warm?" Dave asked while trying to hold his breath.

"Forty times should do the trick!" William answered.

Nick and Dave both let all of the air out of their lungs loudly and at the same time. "Forty?" Nick asked.

"Half an hour or so and you'll be warmer." William reasoned. "Sounds like a nice trade off to me. What else are you going to do while you're shivering in your sleeping bag tonight? Might as well try it!"

The men did try it, more out of fear than belief in William. The only sounds by the campfire in the bitter darkness after dinner was the slow, heavy, and methodical breathing of the men and the kettle spitting water over the flame and the flames hissing back.

"What did Kerouac say about camping?" William asked as he stood up and took a step towards the tent.

"I'm sure you're about to tell us." Nick laconically said.

"Let us sleep by rivers and purify our ears." William said, relishing his role as both the host and the raconteur of this adventure.

The men filed into the tent and squeezed into their respective sleeping bags for the night. It was cramped and crowded, but as the temperatures plummeted to well below zero, the men actually wished there were more people wedged in the tent to try and keep them warm. Other than Nick, no one got much sleep.

Even William, that weathered mountain man and grizzled hiking expert was uncomfortably cold. Just before dawn hit, he crawled out of the tent to try and shake some warmth back into his limbs. As he looked up he momentarily forgot his freezing state of being. William saw that the sky was framed by the black valley sides. He saw a shooting star and then a satellite, winking across the darkness. The only illumination was the curd-yellow moon and the gold-gray flutter of light from the fire. William loved this mix of the old land, high crags, silence, the moon, the fire, and it brought him a feeling of deep calm and connection. He was happy to be here, despite the frigid conditions, with his nephew and two of his best friends. William crawled gingerly back into the tent and his sleeping bag and was able to doze off for just over an hour.

William would have slept longer but Nick had crept over William so he could go outside to answer the call of nature as well as stretch his legs and get the crick out of his back. It was a level of cold that Nick had never experienced before. He felt gelid right down to his bones. Nick found out it wasn't his imagination either that was playing tricks on him, it really was dangerously frigid. When Nick pulled out his sleeping bag it had frozen into a rigid cocoon. Nick propped it against a tree that had a sun beam starting to warm it. Nick then reached for his trousers but they had frozen as well. He stood them up next to his sleeping bag in hopes they would both thaw.

Nick looked up at the sky and said out loud though quietly, "Drunkard's blue." It was an expression from college he and his friends would use to describe the clear sky when they were heading back from the bars or some other nocturnal adventure at dawn and the sun was coming up.

Once everyone woke and exited the tent Nick had cajoled the fire back into life and everyone sat as close as safely possible in hopes of thawing out their extremities as they drank hot tea. An hour later they were back on the trail and continued their hiking onwards and upwards.

Nick and Dave conversed and joked and complained together while Ryder listened to the two men and often laughed or at least smiled at their remarks and quips. William was strangely quiet. His two old friends did not complain about William's sudden silence and instead enjoyed the respite from facts and admonishments. They did not think William to be haughty but sometimes his constant remarks and stories made him seem like he thought he was superior to them. Sure, as a hiker and adventurer he most certainly was and Nick and Dave would readily admit to that. But they were also learned and educated men and were successful in their careers.

"Ryder," Dave said, out of the blue and after all had been silent for a stretch, while huffing and puffing and hiking along, "don't get old. It hurts."

Ryder looked confused so Nick spoke up for his friend, "It's old man talk. Translated it means my feet and legs and back hurt because I spent too much time on the couch with beer and not on a treadmill."

William was not speaking much, if at all, during the first few hours of their hike because he was consumed with fear, and misery. He knew exactly what was wrong and that he was powerless to fix it at that point. Altitude sickness had struck William like a blow from the back of an ax. The sickness of the thin air had left him mute as a fish and sick as a dog. Yet he trundled on.

William knew he had no other recourse than to continue on the path. There was no medicine in his drug kit that could cure him. Some old remedies for altitude sickness included soaking a sponge or cloth in urine and holding it to the nose and mouth. William was not prepared to try that. Even if he could speak, William would not have at that moment because he also felt embarrassed. He thought something like this should happen to a novice like Dave or Nick, or even his young nephew Ryder, but not to an experienced worldwide adventurer like himself.

After an entire morning of trekking at an eleven percent incline the trail mercifully leveled off and for the next hour the men could walk with ease on the path. William thankfully noticed that his head ache started to lessen and his nausea dissipated and soon he was conversing again with his fellow adventurers.

"Are your Cubs going to suck again this year?" Nick asked Dave out of the blue, as they so often would do while hiking.

"Not as bad as your Indians are going to!" Dave snapped back at his friend and then added for good measure, "Chief Wahoo is gay!"

Ryder listened, and laughed and hiked on, clearly entertained by the interactions of these supposedly grown men. Ryder thought, when old friends get together they become young again.

William had no idea who or what a Chief Wahoo was. Ryder was a baseball fan so he knew. Sometimes William felt left out when Dave and Nick would do their shticks, or talk sports. That was always the risk of when there is a group of three people instead of two or four, someone invariably can be made to feel left out whether they really are or not.

Ryder was getting used to Dave and Nick and their humor. Some of it was

'Dad' jokes, like anytime Ryder would say something like, "I'm hungry" or "I'm cold" invariably either Dave or Nick would quickly stick out their hand to shake Ryder's and then say, "I'm (insert name) pleased to meet you!" It never failed to make Ryder laugh which meant those two men would forever do it. William had no children so his jokes didn't trend to that direction of silliness. His comedy was more cerebral.

William had been pretty tight lipped when it came to the exact details of their itinerary, mainly because he wanted the others to be surprised and excited with all the twists and turns of their journey. Plus, he didn't want them to become impatient about their daily destinations i.e. 'are we there yet?' As they sat down to grab a much needed break from hiking and some food William let them know of their proximity to that day's goal. "Men!" William exclaimed jauntily while munching on an apple as the three others looked on through exhausted and dispirited eyes, "we are just a few hours away from warm beds and hot food at the Monastery!"

"Warm what and hot who?" Dave asked, suddenly perking up. Nick's eyes also opened wider.

"I saw on the map that there is a monastery near the base of the mountain. Sometimes they allow Westerners to stay there and they feed them for a small fee." William explained and was very happy to see the joy and hope return to his friend's and nephew's face. It gave him a lift as well.

"Wait, 'sometimes they allow'?" Dave asked skeptically. "So we might get there and they turn us away?"

"Some hope is better than no hope, wouldn't you say?" William asked and Dave thought about it and nodded.

"How much of a fee do you think they'll charge, Uncle?" Ryder asked after he finished his apple and threw it into a deep ravine that bordered the path they were resting on. The Tibetan vistas were legendary and none of them lost sight of that even in their coldest or most weary moments.

"Maybe a dollar, maybe." William answered and the men were duly impressed with the paucity of the fee.

"How much further do you think?" Dave asked. William looked at him, and Nick, and though neither man had a propensity for refusing any pasta meal with alfredo sauce for the past two decades they were both doing exceptionally well on this excursion. He was proud of their effort. William didn't answer quickly because he was debating if he should answer it earnestly or be sarcastic. William despised the 'how much further' question while trekking. He wanted his clients to take their time and enjoy the process.

Nick quickly made fun of his friend by adopting a whiny kid's voice and asked, "Are we there yet Daddy?" Dave glared at Nick but did not say anything back and waited instead for William's response.

"A couple of hours, tops. We will be there before dusk." William promised and the men stood and began to hike towards a possible night of hot food and a comfortable, and more importantly warm, bed.

The path took a slight down slope and then they were walking through another forest of trees. This blocked the sunshine from warming them but it also blocked the wind from cooling them so it was a net zero difference in temperature. The change of scenery was refreshing and it put yet another bounce into their steps. All were again quiet though. Each person was deep in their own thoughts. The quiet contemplation this trip afforded each man was quite an unexpected benefit.

Ryder tried to figure out the time differences between Tibet and Florida and what Leanne was probably doing at that exact moment. Whatever it was that she was up to, he prayed that she still loved him as much as she did when he left. The one thing that this trip had yet to alter, at this point any way, was his fixation on her and their relationship. At sixteen he had very little perspective. He only knew he had never dreamt in his life he would be this happy with another person or feel so important.

Finally they emerged from an arch in the trees and right upon them was the monastery, perched just on the brink of a ravine, And right on top of the monastery, it seemed, was the mountain itself. The monastery looked like it was the size of a dot compared to the towering mountain that rose behind it. The slope and the trees had hidden the mountain from those four all morning but now here it was standing up straight and tall in all its glory to wish them a good afternoon!

The men fought an urge to hurry straight to the monastery and the promised delicacies and comforts of mattresses and pillows and instead they sat quietly on a grass bank in the sunlight near the holy place. William dug out a camera from his rucksack and handed it to Ryder.

"Here." Uncle William said to his nephew. "Can you take a picture of three old men in front of a mountain?"

"Sure! Where are they? I don't see any old men!" Ryder said with a smile and the three men smiled back at his compliment.

"Brown nose!" Nick said with a smile to Ryder.

William reached out his arms and Nick stood under his left arm while Dave stood under William's right and they smiled brightly and proudly as Ryder snapped the picture.

"Maybe one more in case your thumb was in the way!" Nick joked. The men stood still with their arms interlocked. Ryder thought they all just wanted an excuse to stand close together and bask in their friendship and accomplishment. Ryder squinted through the lens and took one more picture and then handed the camera back to his uncle who then carefully placed it in a padded spot inside his rucksack.

"Wait, what about one with Ryder?" Nick asked.

William deliberated and then shook his head, "No, let's just get another one when we come back down." It was a chore to pack and unpack the camera from the padded spot in his rucksack.

"No, come on, you never know, we might forget or -" Nick argued and then

Dave interrupted his friend and joined in the cajoling.

"Or your camera breaks." Dave added.

"Or freezes." Nick added to Dave's add.

"Or you freeze." Dave said and at that point William knew it would be futile to argue with them any longer.

"Ok, ok, fine!" William knelt and carefully took out his camera and then set it up on a knee high flat rock. He tinkered with it for a spell until he was satisfied it was perfect and ready to be activated. "I have this feature, if you press this button it waits five seconds and then it snaps the picture. We can all be in it!"

"Have Ryder do it," Nick explained, "none of us are fast enough to get into position in five seconds!"

"Five seconds," Dave replied, "Nick, you couldn't get there in five minutes!"

"True, you're both true." William said and motioned for his nephew to come over and see how this feature worked. Once shown, Ryder crouched down and looked at the three men, all standing again with their arms around each other. "Press it and run here!"

Ryder did press the button and was about to run but he then tripped on an unseen rock and was about to fall on his face when Nick moved swiftly, caught him, and then lifted him up and turned him into the direction of the camera so when it snapped those two were facing it! At the same time Dave and William were looking at Ryder and Nick in utter amazement. It was a once in a lifetime shot especially with Minya Konka rising behind them in the frame. None of the men would know how amazing that picture was until months later when it was developed stateside.

The men then put their rucksacks back onto their shoulders and walked into the courtyard of the monastery. There was nobody around. There were two main buildings in the compound and both were adorned with many colorful prayer flags and bronze prayer wheels. The windows and doorways of both of the buildings were facing the mountain. Racks of incense sticks smoldered with rings of orange fire creeping down them while blue smoke coiled up into the still air.

In the middle of the dusty and empty compound was a table with four chairs around it, almost as though they knew four people were going to arrive that morning. The men walked over to the table and chairs and after wearily taking their sacks off of their backs they gratefully sat down. The wind provided the only sound. The men looked at each other, their eyes darting from a friend to an empty building and back to another friend. Their expressions asked what the next move was even if their mouths did not open.

"Was there a vacancy sign on?" Nick asked but none answered or even laughed at his quip. They were too tense.

When the men felt like they could not take any more silence or uncertainty a Tibetan lady with a lined face that comes from six decades of living in such windy and exposed conditions walked up to the men and then looked them over. She nodded without smiling. The men nodded back and William spoke up and said with a beaming smile, "Namaste." The reaction was not what he hoped for, she only nodded again and then walked away and disappeared into the same building she had emerged from only a minute before.

"Do we leave?" Dave asked.

"Let's find out, I'm not sure yet." William answered and they sat and waited for her to emerge again.

Minutes passed by slowly as they waited and wondered if they were welcome there or if they needed to be moving on and pitching their tent and spending an even colder night amidst the elements.

The lady walked out of the same building but this time she was holding a plate and a pitcher of a yellow liquid. She placed them on the table, nodded matter of factly, and then walked away to the other building on the grounds.

The men looked on the plate and saw that she brought them cookies and inside the pitcher appeared to be a type of lemonade. "This is a good sign!"

William proclaimed but then recanted a bit. "I think."

"Best cookie I ever had!" Ryder said upon biting into it. He was the first of them to try one. "Coconut wafer cookie!"

"You do love coconut!" Uncle William said to his nephew and then also took a bite of the cookie and his moan clearly meant he also loved the taste. Nick and Dave then did the same and had the same reaction of delight.

Nick then reached for the pitcher and poured a bit of the liquid contents into Williams' ornate white pottery cup and asked, "Some urine for you?" That was the color it appeared most like. William tasted it and looked relieved.

"Nope, lemonade." William said just as the lady exited another doorway of the building and this time was carrying two mattresses. She walked by them after giving them a perfunctory glance.

"So are we welcome here or not?" Dave asked in between bites of the cookie and gulps of the lemonade.

"Still too early to tell, but by the looks of what she was carrying I think she's getting our rooms ready." William deduced. The men sat and continued to eat in the windy yet relaxing conditions of the monastery.

The men then heard some children's laughter and then over the ridge saw five young boys, all with shaved heads and red robes coming near their way. The boys were being trained in ways of their religion and while it could be arduous and time consuming work they had a playful and light way about them of all children around the world.

The boys laughed and waved after the men first waved a hello to them. William offered up a joyful, "Namaste!" and the five boys all returned his salutation. They then walked to the first building the older lady had appeared from and they were soon gone from view.

Within seconds from that happening the lady appeared again and walked across the compound with just a scant nod in the Americans direction. A minute later she appeared again with two more mattresses.

"Looks like we're 'in like Flynn' friends" William said while both smiling and chewing and now sitting back in his chair. Nick, Dave, and Ryder now all also felt relaxed and fully enjoyed their impromptu feast.

The lady then reappeared and motioned for them to follow her into what appeared to be the auxiliary building. It was square shaped and not quite as large nor ornate as the main building. The men rose and followed her and upon entering the building noticed a labyrinth of heavy wooden doors that bordered a square room of windows in the very middle of the structure. The men looked inside the windows and saw a colorfully adorned room with many musical instruments and religious statues situated about.

She stopped and opened one of the heavy, wooden doors and made way for the men to enter the room. They saw four beds, each on a corner, and that was it. Barren but warm and comfortable compared to the hard, cold, and unforgiving ground of the mountainous tundra that had been sleeping on.

The lady then made a motion of washing her hands and when William smiled, nodded, and said, "Yes!" She then took them to where the bathroom resided. It was outside and just around the corner. A plastic lined hole sat where a traditional western toilet would have normally been.

She then touched her wrist and held up two fingers. The men looked confused at what she was trying to convey. She then tapped her wrist again, held up the same two fingers, but this time then also made a motion of a spoon or fork feeding her mouth. "I think we will eat in two hours." William deduced and then nodded and smiled to her to show her he understood her pantomime.

The men lounged on their mattresses and Dave even dozed off to sleep. Ryder started to write Leanne a letter and began it by first declaring his undying love for her and after those three pages were filled he then wrote about their current day's trekking adventures. Nick and William were almost too tired to think and simply enjoyed the pleasure of having their eyes closed and not freezing or moving.

By the time the lady came back to summon the men for dinner it was both dark and very cold again. As they walked across the compound to the main building they braced themselves against the wind and tried not to trip on any unseen obstacles. Once they opened the door they entered a large rectangular room that was lined on the outer walls with comfortable and cushy pillows and at the head of the room was a throne like structure that was currently unoccupied. At the opposite end of the room from the throne was a huge cast iron wood stove. The lady motioned for the men to sit on the pillows while she then bowed down and opened the glass door to the wood stove and began to insert paper and kindling into it.

"Can I help?" Nick asked the lady while the other three sat down and they all noticed the wonderful fragrances of warm and delicious food wafting through the closed door to what appeared to be the kitchen area.

"Come on baby, light my fire." Dave sang, trying to sound like Jim Morrison of The Doors.

The lady, of course, had not a clue of what Dave sang nor of what Nick asked but the way he used his hands he conveyed the point to her and she smiled and nodded. Nick began to put the kindling in just so, giving each plenty of air to catch fire easily with. When the lady handed him a log, Nick pretended it was so heavy that it knocked him over and he fell onto the floor. It was a straight old fashioned silent movie comedy bit from the Charlie Chaplin era but the lady laughed loudly nonetheless.

While Nick and the lady worked on getting the fire started another door swung open and a short and slightly rotund man of maybe fifty years old entered the room. He wore a blue sweatshirt, tan corduroy pants, and a short knitted blue ski hat on his head.

"Hello." He said in slightly fractured yet perfectly passable English, "It is nice to meet you. I am the guru."

***

For the pomp and circumstance of such a lofty title, the men thought, the 'guru' was surprisingly down to earth. He spoke mostly of how he visited New York City twice in the past decade and that accounted for his ability to converse somewhat in English. The guru mostly asked the men many questions about themselves. Personal questions were followed by more and deeper delving questions.

Dave spoke openly about his dissolving marriage. Nick talked of how he was occasionally apt to take his family for granted. William ventured that he was too cavalier with his romances. Ryder lamented that maybe he was not a good enough son in that he kept his room untidy. The other three men laughed at Ryder's response. What is so bad about an untidy room compared to what they were going through? The guru hooked onto that.

"No, my friends," the guru said addressing the three older men, "do not laugh at Ryder. Perspective. He is young, a tidy room might be a large factor. He knows his mother is not happy about it. He is conscious of her unhappiness. Consciousness is desire. And desire is eternity, with life and death flowing through it - life and death, all one and the same thing, coming and going, coming and going."

Dave whispered to Nick, "That's like, kinda deep."

Nick whispered back, "Yes. My deepest thought usually is 'hey hey mama, say the way you move, gonna make you sweat, gonna make you groove." Both men then made a little air guitar motion and then laughed quietly about it.

"I think that would be Karim's deepest thought as well!" Dave said about their driver who wore the Led Zeppelin jacket. They then laughed louder. The two men looked around and then thought they should hide their laughter because it might be deemed disrespectful to the guru. He thought otherwise.

"The Maharishi Yogi says the highest state is laughter. I agree." The guru said and looked at the men. He felt he needed to explain more. "I've also heard that laughter is carbonated holiness. We need to laugh, never hide it. We don't laugh because we're happy, we're happy because we laugh."

As the men pondered that nugget of philosophy dinner was brought into that room and the men gathered at the table. Dal bhat was on everyone's plate and with the extra turmeric the lady put into it, the taste was memorable.

The conversation went back to a light and airy way until Dave spoke of being nervous that his impending divorce would leave him poor.

Here the guru leaned into the table with his elbows and looked deep into Dave's eyes and just stared for a beat before speaking to him. "The horror of poverty is the hopelessness of forever being imprisoned by it. The horror of poverty is in its sense of confinement." With that being said, the guru went back to his dinner with a smiling face.

No more deep discussions were to be had that night with the three older men but the guru did have some advice for Ryder and his burgeoning love affair with Leanne back in the United States. "The key to a long lasting loving relationship is empathy and selflessness. If you are both of these things, you will have a clean slate no matter what happens. You cannot control anything but your own actions so keep them focused on others. Do your honest best and then you rest." The men, laying on the pillows that surrounded the room, laid comfortably in the soothing dry heat and listened to this advice that Ryder received from the guru and all three in their minds agreed that it was sound and essential. All three also agreed that none of them succeeded in living that way.

***

The four Americans were more than an hour on the upward and basically pathless terrain before any of them spoke of anything really consequential. "Uncle William, can we go back to that monastery after we climb this mountain when we come down?" Ryder asked, clearly enamored of the place.

"Yes, what do you think, William? Would that work?" Dave asked, as he was also touched by his experience there.

"I wish, but that's the opposite direction that we're leaving from." William answered and then added, "And remember, we're not climbing the mountain, per se, we're not going to the summit. We're going to do a kora of it." The men digested William's news and then they walked on silently, as silently as old friends can walk. There were many comments, asides, routines that they engaged in while walking. Most came out of nowhere. They would spout dialogue from a favorite old movie. Sometimes it would be dialogue from a particularly terrible movie they loved because it was so bad. Sometimes there were just sounds they shared. Dave would make a high pitched grunt and Nick would follow with the same as would William. Ryder did not know what it meant or its origins, he just knew it further bonded these buddies of many decades.

The topography changed to a maze of boulders and melt-streams. They were now following a river. William hoped it was the correct one. The rivers kept channeling off into several directions. The shifting ice below many areas caused the landscape to keep changing. The trip now became physically taxing and it was good they had worked their muscles so aptly the previous week. The men rock-hopped between lumps of white rocks as large as desks, and crossed the bigger streams by wading, or improvising bridges from tree trunks. It was slow going and progress was measured by what the eye could see ahead, not in kilometers. A couple of slips caused a few scrapes and a small collection of bloody shins and knees but nothing major.

William pointed out a small herd of musk deer as they crossed the main Konka moraine and the men stopped and gratefully rested and watched. Later that hour William then bent down and traced with his finger the pug marks left in the gray silt by what he thought looked like a large feline, most likely the reclusive snow leopard.

"Think we'll see one of those, William? I've never seen one of those!" Nick exclaimed excitedly.

William threw cold water on his friend's enthusiasm, "I haven't either. Most people haven't."

William guided them to now follow the route that bordered the biggest river and all four were sweating despite the below freezing temperatures. The men passed and sometimes had to climb over boulders that were covered with ivory-colored ice that resembled a dripping from a church's wax candles. At a turn of the river where the rapids made a deafening roar, a flock of finches were startled by the men's sudden approach and gusted up from the river-shore with shrill cries.

The trail then resumed its upward trajectory. A few hours of this and William turned and went around a bend of boulders when he saw a slight opening. He stopped and peered into the narrow passageway. The others stopped and caught their breath while he did this. He then waved them over and disappeared into the granite doorway.

The rock threshold led to a gorge that opened up to a secret valley. As far as the men could see there was an expanse of undulating grassland for a couple of miles! It was a pasturage where countless animals lived unmolested in this sanctuary for time immemorial. Due to it being inaccessible to local herdsmen and its entryway hidden from hikers and pilgrims, the men were now in a lost world of botanical riches.

Giant cliffs of their mountain they were hiking on rose sheer and forbidding in true Tibetan style, but, bounding the glacier on the right-hand side, beyond a well-defined lateral moraine, beheld a dream landscape for the men to frolic in and rest amongst.

Though not late in the day, William made an executive decision that they would camp there for the night. With the trees in abundance, the men would have a roaring fire to cook on and rest close to.

As Ryder gathered the firewood and Dave and Nick fastened the tent spikes, William had some thoughts that at first he thought he would keep to himself so the others would not ridicule him Then he thought about it and didn't much care if they did, he was going to share what he was feeling as he surveyed that secret paradise.

"This surpasses any blissful dream I ever had as a child, this magical valley we're in." William stated as the others stopped doing their chores and simply listened. "We just might be the first humans to ever be here."

The others pondered the enormity of that last statement and it brought to the surface how amazing this moment really was.

"We're free to wander wherever we wish," William continued, "and discover this hitherto unrevealed glory of Nature. This is a dream come true only even better than I have ever dreamed. How many childish fancies can be said, in this age of disillusionment?"

Wholly uncynical, Nick added, "I would have paid a million dollars for this. It's worth more than a million dollars. Once in a lifetime!"

"Exactly. There are few treasures of more lasting worth than this experience. Maybe there are none." William said and Dave and Ryder nodded.

"Amen." Nick said, clearly still in awe of where they were.

An hour later their bonfire was huge, warming, and very bright as the flames threatened to lick the sky.

It was at these bonfires that Ryder learned the most about his Uncle William and his two best friends. The talk would meander this way and that way, sometimes deep and meaningful and other times just jovial or even full of non-sequiturs. Tonight was no exception. Following the reverential words about their surroundings Nick then offered up this nugget of information about himself in the form of a question to the group, "Have any of you sat on your heel?" Nick's eyes timidly waited for an answer as he felt he might have overshared an especially embarrassing detail.

Surprisingly, Ryder spoke up, "You mean to keep from - " Ryder thought twice about what he was going to say and became silent.

"What? What?" Nick asked excitedly.

Ryder hesitated but then went ahead with his thoughts, "When I was a kid and we were all out playing and I had to go to the bathroom, I mean really go, where I couldn't just pee on a tree, I would -" Ryder's voice trailed off as he thought better of what he was going to share. Nick was on the edge of his seat while the other two men had no idea where this conversation was heading.

"You would what?" Nick asked Ryder eagerly, hoping for a kindred spirit.

"I would sit on my heel a certain way and it would just go away, I wouldn't have to go in and go to the bathroom, I could keep playing."

"Yes! No way, Ryder! I never thought I'd meet another soul that did that too!" Nick exclaimed, both pleased and vindicated. Ryder smiled brightly while the other two men groaned and uttered derisive comments.

"Oh, yeah right, tell me you don't have something weird and hidden in your depths!" Nick said to the two scoffing men. "William, didn't you tell me you used to bite your toenails when you were a kid?"

All eyes turned to William, the man who tried to maintain an air of sophistication.

"You're among friends, Willy Boy." Dave said assuringly.

"Fine. I did." William admitted.

"That's really gross!" Nick declared and laughed. "I mean, I'm proud of you for admitting it but that's really disgusting! How old were you when you stopped biting your toenails?" Nick asked.

William lowered his eyes and made the men wait for a couple of moments and then spoke, "Occasionally, when I was still limber enough, I would do that into my, I don't know, maybe mid-twenties."

The three others roared in laughter and grossed out reactions.

When the campfire was quiet again, save the crackling of the firewood, Dave spoke. "If you kick me in a certain part of my back, I can always fart."

The men scoffed and reacted with laughter and doubt but when Dave lay down on the ground and kind of flipped his legs over his head and asked Nick to kick him in a specific area of his back, sure enough, he did fart, and loudly!

Exclamations of "No way!" and "I'm so impressed" mixed around the campfire along with, "Gross!"

Once the noise settled down again, all eyes were on Ryder. He did not want to say a word but they expected him to share something he felt was embarrassing or at least very private and as yet unshared with anyone else.

"Well?" Dave asked.

"Oh, leave the kid alone, he already admitted the 'sitting on the heel' thing!" Nick said, rising to Ryder's defense. "Maybe he's not as weird as we are." Nick paused and then added, "Yet!"

Everyone laughed and then Ryder finally spoke. "Ok," the teenager said while taking a deep breath and mustering up his courage, "this year, I have had -" Ryder silently counted on his fingers and then spoke again, "four firsts with a girl. All the same girl. The first was French kissing and the other three…that's all I'm going to say!" Ryder hoped Leanne would not mind that he shared that facet of their relationship. Being so young they really were learning about love together.

William and Nick patted Ryder on the shoulder and Dave gave him an enthusiastic thumbs up and all was right with their world.

The dinner and the campfire were the best of the trip and the sleep they all enjoyed was the deepest yet.

The next morning they were sad to leave their personal paradise but at the same time, being a shared delight, they knew they would remember it always.

The men took one last look around and exited their Shangri-La.

"Or is it a Shambala?" Dave asked and began to sing that Doobie Brothers song. Nick then joined him singing and then so did William, all three men smiling broadly. Ryder did not know the words but added his voice nonetheless when they joyfully sang the high notes of the refrain

Rejuvenated, the hiking commenced. It was a tough climb that day.

The men continued to climb ever higher and reached the lower walls of the north-west ridge and stopped in the afternoon sunshine to eat their lunch and drink their thirst quenching water from their canteens. It had been a long day and William knew despite the beauty of their surroundings they shouldn't stay at this spot too long. As they ascended William thought he saw a huge ice bulge hundreds of yards across above the very spot they were resting. The men were worn out or he would have pushed them further. William thought the bulging snowfields and desperate fall-lines should hold long enough for them to gain their strength back from some food and drinks.

"How does this kora work?" Nick asked with barely a sound coming out of his oxygen depleted lungs. Nick took a long draw of water, coughed, and then drank some more. He had to repeat himself to be heard.

"We go around the mountain." William answered and was surprised at how dry his throat was and how his chest and lungs felt like they were being crushed by an invisible two-handed giant.

"But what was all that ambulating stuff?" Nick asked, taking a labored breath in between every word.

Ryder was wondering the same thing but all he could do at the moment was lean against the ice wall and close his eyes. He wished he weighed more than the 136 pounds he started the trip at, it might have made carrying such a heavy rucksack easier. With all the strenuous hiking and scrambling he had been doing the past week he doubted he even weighed 130 pounds any more. 'Will Leanne think I'm too skinny now?' Ryder thought to himself and, now worried, made a note to eat more.

"There is circumambulating," William replied, also struggling for his breath but trying not to show his discomfort to the others, "and that is a mind boggling religious pilgrimage. Since the 1200s, Buddhist pilgrims have been walking and riding to the mountain. That's what we've done."

"Hooray for us!" Nick said trying to muster up some positive spirit in his voice but it still sounded flat to him.

"Yes, hooray for us." William said with a smile and appreciated his friend's good nature despite such trying circumstances. William took a bite of his bread roll and then continued, "The circumambulate is when these pilgrims bend, kneel, lie face down, mark the earth with their fingers, rise, pray, shuffle forwards to the finger marks, bend, kneel…and do it all over again! For thirty-two miles! The entire massif!"

The other three men were appropriately impressed and even a little confused on how or why anyone would partake in such an endeavor.

"I told you, it's their sacred mountain. They're fervently committed to living the practices of their devotion." William reasoned. "Wouldn't you visit Heaven if you could? Wouldn't you do anything to honor a god that let you? A god that put such a beautiful, snow-covered temple that you could visit, and circumambulate? Wouldn't you?"

The men thought about their own personal levels of devotion to their own personal gods and or religions.

Ryder's religion, being just sixteen years old, was whatever his parents impressed upon him. That was Catholicism. Though he prayed pretty much every night he never gave it much thought. It was always the same words, night after night. The 'Our Father', a couple of 'Hail Mary's', and then a plea to be forgiven for whatever sins he might have committed that day. One possible sin he never asked forgiveness for was the premarital physical relations he reveled in with Leanne. They were both teaching each other at that tender age and neither felt a pang of guilt about any of it.

Dave was also raised Catholic and his sense of guilt was very strong and ingrained into his psyche. He knew divorce was wrong. He knew why he was getting divorced was wrong and a sin. He also knew there was no going back. The priests said he was forgiven every Saturday evening that he went to confession and then Mass so he hoped it to be true. What choice did he have at this point?

Nick was raised as a Christian Orthodox and until he was almost twenty attended his Serbian Orthodox Church in the suburb of Cleveland that he grew up in. Once college started his church attendance plummeted and was now non-existent. He never really thought about it much and let his wife raise their daughter as a Lutheran and was fine with it just as long as he could sleep in Sunday while they were gone.

William liked to say he was a recovering Catholic and purged himself the best he could of the guilt genes that seemed to have clutched his soul as a youth. He now bowed at the altar of women that were considerably younger than he was and if he thought maybe he should reform and repent, well, there was always time for that some day.

Within barely two seconds of a rumble that resembled a freight train bearing down on them to warn them, the ice sheet above them cracked. An avalanche of several tons of rocks and ice and snow plunged towards them as they paused from their respite of water and food and looked upwards, unbelieving that the monstrous sound they heard had anything to do with them. The other three thought it might be thunder that they were hearing. All except William, he knew exactly what was happening and worse, what was about to happen to them as they sat exposed to the mountain's wrath.

***

Forget bears, nothing is more dangerous in the mountains than avalanches. Since 1784 there have been 82 fatal human/bear conflicts in North America. In the entire world there are an average 40 deaths a year from bears. There are an average 100,000 avalanches per year in the United States alone and that does not even make the top five for countries in the world. The number of people that die from avalanches per year is over 150.

Avalanches can weigh over a million pounds and travel faster than 320 kilometers or 200 miles per hour. As an avalanche speeds down a mountain it may compress the air below it and create winds that could blow a house apart, breaking windows, splintering doors, and blowing off the roof.

A single avalanche in Yungay, Peru in 1970 destroyed the town and killed 18,000 people. No single bear has ever killed 18,000 people.

***

William knew from experience that if an avalanche hits and covers you in snow you need to punch your hand up to give yourself some breathing room. There is no way a person can wrangle their body out of the snowpack, because a human body is three times more dense than the snow itself. Swimming up and out of the snow is mostly a pipedream of the victims. Once the avalanche stops moving it settles like concrete and bodily movement is impossible. People usually die in an avalanche from suffocation.

As the ice, rocks, and snow began to rain down on him, William thrust his arms upwards so that he would be able to have them free to punch upwards and be able to breath. Within seconds of doing this two different rocks, each no bigger than seven inches in circumference, battered and broke three of his ribs. He then lowered his arms and turned around and away from the top of the mountain and cradled his head in arms so any rocks that struck him would only smash into his feet or back.

The first blast of debris that came down hit Ryder from the side and top and he was thrown immediately three lengths of his body to the southwest of where he had been previously resting. This placed him behind a large boulder which at first seemed like a safe place to be. A lot of the ice and rock missiles were being blocked by the rock which was the size of a large refrigerator. But if enough snow came down that mountain and pushed the boulder over it would crush Ryder to death.

Dave was pelted with many rocks and ice balls and then was carried by the rushing snow 30 meters down the mountain where he slammed into a boulder and broke his back in several places. Two in his cervical vertebrae, three in his thoracic vertebrae, and two more in his lumbar vertebrae were instantly fractured. The C6 and C7 vertebrae were a burst fracture as they broke into multiple pieces in all directions. As loud as Dave lay screaming in pain the avalanche was louder and none of his friends heard him.

Nick heard the loud sound of the avalanche and then a second later he heard nothing. An ice bullet struck and broke his neck. His C1-C3 vertebrae, the ones that contain nerves that help him breath, were destroyed and thus the neurological supply to his respiratory muscles were compromised and led to respiratory failure.

William saw his lifelong friend get pummeled with the debris and then saw the blood jump from just below his neck. As William tried to crawl over through the pain of his own broken ribs he saw Nick open his eyes and look right at him. William made it to Nick and cradled his buddy's head in his arms just as Nick took his last breath and died. William could not comprehend that this just happened. He had never had never had a client that he guided die, or even get seriously injured. The fact that the first time it happened was to one of his best friends made his heart and soul clenched tightly and burned with regret and anguish. All that medical training, the CPR training, the basic life support training, the advanced life support training, all meant nothing. This was what he was supposed to be good at, his thing, his niche, his expertise. Instead, he felt useless and impotent to help his friend in any way. William then held his friend tightly and just kept repeating one word over and over and over, "No!"

***

Ryder still didn't quite comprehend exactly what was happening to him and what had happened to his three traveling partners. He didn't know how he was going to survive this onslaught of projectiles that were jetting down the mountain. The snow was quickly engulfing him like it was water. Before he knew it, the snow was up to his neck and still rising. That is when he heard, "Punch your arms up!" And so he did. And as the snow now covered his face he had room to breath even as everything became very dark and suddenly quiet. Ryder thought, hoped, it was just a dream.

***

Dave was no longer screaming in pain. He was no longer making any sound.

When Dave was a child his mother used to take him shopping for clothes, which he dreaded. It was not just because he wanted to be playing with his friends instead of being led by his hand from store to store looking for slacks, but because invariably his mother would ask one of the salesmen, "Where is your husky section for my boy?"

The husky section. Back in that era when most humans were in pretty good shape and childhood obesity or even chubbiness was extremely rare, Dave's physique warranted a trip to the 'husky section'. William and Nick loved when Dave would regale them with his childhood stories. He was a natural comedian and storyteller. Football and fiance were his two passions as he grew into a teenager. One helped him get into better shape physically and the other helped him grow financially.

Improving physically and financially helped him find the woman that he chose to marry. He would have been a great husband too, had he not chosen so poorly. Betsy, or 'B' as he liked to call her, was his worst audience. Dave loved a good crowd for his storytelling and shticks, B was not that. She actually was an anti-audience and just didn't laugh but would tell Dave either how unfunny he was or that she already heard him say that certain quip before.

Dave needed an audience, and validation, which he understood to be the same as intimacy and endearment, and so he looked elsewhere for it to feel good about himself. Twenty years later he was separated, adrift, and wondering why simple things had to be so difficult and funny things so sad. He had hoped the beauty and grandeur of the mountains would whisper to him some clarity.

***

Thanks to the instruction Ryder got, he was now free of the snow pack that threatened to suffocate him. He lay on his back, breathing heavily, and thought about what he should do next. "Go to Dave." Ryder heard and then he opened his eyes, sat upright, and looked in every direction until he saw the man motionless further down the ravine.

Ryder was very fortunate. All that his body had to show from the terror of the avalanche was a few scrapes and a couple of blots of blood. Nothing on him was broken, fractured, or punctured.

Ryder scrambled over the snow and scree until he was at Dave's side. Ryder had no medical training and was the least medically inclined person he knew. Now Leanne on the other hand, she loved medicine and wanted to be a doctor someday. Leanne. His mind drifted to her and he again lamented being out on this injurious mountain on this deadly day instead of being home with her. "Check if he is breathing." Ryder heard the command and then lowered his ear to Dave's chest.

***

It took awhile for William to compose himself and get his thoughts back on safety and survival for his nephew and friend. He looked down the ravine and could see his nephew next to Dave. He couldn't see much more from his vantage point. Seeing his nephew moving, William figured at least he was alright for the time being. He couldn't tell Daves' condition because his friend was laying down and not moving.

William went into his rucksack and took out his sleeping bag and unfurled it. He then began to cry again, and then the crying turned into weeping and sobbing as he looked down on his deceased friend Nick. He then lifted Nick's head and placed it gently onto the sleeping bag. William, through a copious amount of tears, then completely covered Nick in his sleeping bag and then zippered it to the top. Once he was through doing that, William slowly and carefully made his way down the ravine to where Ryder and Dave were located. William feared the worst for another friend of his as he slipped his way to them.

***

When William first heard the news he raised his drink, a high ball, and exclaimed, "Well, Jimmy Carter finally did something right!" It was September of 1979 and the previous week, William had been leading a group of Japanese automobile executives up Mt. Kilimanjaro in Tanzania, Africa. He was relaxing in the piano lounge of the Hotel Mizingani Seafront hotel in the Malindi district of Tanzania. A slurry rendition of "Mack the Knife" was being warbled by the Filipino pianist when an old acquaintance strode up to William and exclaimed, "The Chinese are letting climbers climb in Tibet again!"

It was a long time in the making.

Following World War Two there was a violent internal war in China that was finally won by the Communist Party in 1949. It was, though, a climber's paradise. With more land mass than any other country on Earth except for Russia and Canada and containing seven peaks over 8000 meters high and another nearly 12,000 mountains, what adventurer and mountaineer wouldn't want to explore China, and it's neighbor Tibet?

But then in 1950 Tibet was no longer China's neighbor, it was its prisoner, its possession. China invaded Tibet on the pretext that it was liberating that country from Western domination. At the time of the invasion there were a total of five Westerners in Tibet. Tibet appealed for international assistance but the United States had already given China renewed assurances of its recognition of China's de jure sovereignty or suzerainty over Tibet. Britain had pulled out of India so it no longer had a border it wanted to protect. Also, after the Second

World War and the loss of life and hardship it had caused, Great Britain had no stomach to bleed further in such a far off land that provided no practical benefits. The United Nations later condemned China's invasion on three separate occasions but neither it, nor any other country was willing to offer Tibet meaningful help.

The Chinese brutalized the Tibetans into submission and tried to crush the Buddhist religion that lay at the heart of Tibetan society. At the time of the invasion there were about six thousand monasteries in Tibet, all but a dozen were razed. The Chinese burned ancient Tibetan texts, destroyed libraries, smashed thousands of religious relics, and shipped hundreds of tons of crafted Tibetan metals to Beijing, where they were melted down. The Chinese also committed genocide on a scale that matched some of the worst atrocities seen in the twentieth century. Hundreds of thousands of Tibetans were beaten, imprisoned, enslaved, tortured, shot, and starved. In total, the Chinese killed an estimated 1,200,000 Tibetans. Once their neighbors. Not very neighborly.

As the world started to take notice of these ghastly atrocities, China thought better about how their government looked and so they sent a delegation first to Tibet and then to the United States towards the end of the 1970s. The Carter administration pressured them to play nice with their bloodied neighbor and thereafter a declaration was made that foreign climbers could once again try to stand atop their many marvelous summits. This is the news that William heard and celebrated in that African piano bar.

William's mind quickly went to his two best friends from college. He had seen very little of them in the past decade but what he knew about them was not promising. Dave was struggling through a separation and Nick was struggling through middle age. Neither was thriving physically nor emotionally. William thought an excursion to a mountain would do the trick, and a goal of not reaching the summit but simply enjoying the sights and the strenuous exertions would be perfect.

William made some calls to old friends and government officials, he filled out requests and permits. He then coaxed, begged, and bribed his two old friends to embark on this journey with them. William wore them down and they finally acquiesced. And now, because he wouldn't take 'no' for an answer, this disaster happened to his two best friends, as well as his sixteen year old nephew.

***

Ryder now regretted knowing nothing about first aid. His favorite show on television was MASH, which was about surgeons during the Korean War, but he knew that would not help him in any way now. "Loosen his scarf and prop him up." Ryder heard and then obeyed the command. He could faintly hear Dave struggling to breath. "Give him some water." Ryder did as he was told.

***

Before he fully closed the sleeping bag zipper, William cut a large swath of Nick's colorful scarf off of him. William then put the piece of scarf into his pocket and fastened that closed. William then finished zipping Nick's body into his sleeping bag as a burial wrap and then stood up and looked down the ravine at Ryder and Dave.

"I did what you said to do!" Ryder yelled up to his uncle who was confused by what his nephew meant.

William then bent down and tried to move Nick's body but he was heavier than he expected. William hated to do this, but he called down to his young nephew to help him. "Ryder, come up here quickly!"

Ryder scrambled up the slope and was at his uncle's side within a minute. "Uncle, poor Dave is - "

"I know, I saw. But please help me first." William asked, motioning down to the sleeping bag with his eyes.

"Is Nick hurt badly?" Ryder asked, not knowing.

William did not know how to answer, he couldn't meet his nephew's gaze. William took a long breath and slowly let it out and his cracked ribs led him to cough. And then cough some more. He spit some blood out of his mouth while his nephew looked on and waited for his question to be answered. "Our buddy Nick is dead."

Ryder stared at his uncle with unbelieving eyes as the color drained from the young man's face.

"He didn't suffer much, he was killed instantly. Help me bring his body to that crevice so we can bury him properly."

"Bury him?" Ryder asked as his uncle's words still did not sink properly in. "Wait, aren't we going to take him home? Bury him at home? Won't his wife and daughter want to see him and pray - "

"Ryder," William said less patiently than he wanted, "we'll be lucky to get off this mountain alive if we're not careful, there is no way we could bring his body down too." William tried to soften his voice, "We have to be safe. I have to get you home alive and well to my sister, and that girlfriend of yours!" William tried to smile but his face refused. Ryder looked lost and devastated.

"Ok, Uncle." Ryder answered, though clearly still not getting the impact of everything that had just happened.

"Let's take him over there." William said, pointing to a deep crevasse less than a third of a football field away. "Then we have to help Dave." It was hard work but they did it as quickly as they could.

As they stood over the deep hole with Nick's body on the edge in a sleeping bag, William spoke, "I love you, pal, and always will. And I am so sorry I got you killed. Please forgive me. God bless your sweet soul." Tears poured down both William and Ryder's faces' and they stood motionless while the wind blew and the cold stung. Small flakes of snow began to blow and thus made William regain his direction. William remembered a bit of an old Bible verse from Psalm

23 and said it as he stood over the body of his dear friend, "The Lord is my shepherd," he forgot a few of the words but continued, "He guides me along the right paths for his name's sake." William paused as he now tried to compose himself. "Goodbye my Nicky." William then rolled the sleeping bag with Nick's body in it over and into the deep tomb of the crevasse.

***

The snow started to come down heavier. That would make sense there in the Himalaya. The name, properly used always in the singular, is an ancient Sanskrit compound meaning "abode of snow" (Hima, snow; alaya, abode).

Currently, and for the past many millennia, India has been plowing into Tibet at the breakneck speed of five centimeters a year and lifts the Himalaya by as much as a centimeter every twelve months or so. Yes, the mountains are still getting taller! The fastest rising mountain is Nanga Parbat (26,659ft/8126m) on the far western extremity of the Himalaya and will one day stand taller than Mt. Everest.

All of this pushing up in this part of the world started one hundred twenty million years ago when the Indian land mass broke free of the colossal Mesozoic continent of Gondwana and began to drift northward at an astonishing average speed of sixteen centimeters a year. About forty-five million years ago it crossed the equator and collided with the submerged edge of Eurasia along a front of about fifteen hundred miles. Much of the dense ocean floor north of India plunged into the earth's mantle and disappeared beneath a line of now extinct volcanoes. As the inexorable collision continued and completely closed the intervening sea, the lighter sedimentary rocks of India and Tibet had nowhere to go but up. There have been fossils found on the summit of Mt. Everest with sea creatures in them! This collision created the highest mountain range on earth, the Himalaya. The range is one thousand five hundred miles long and in a geological sense is very much alive and comprises the greatest geophysical feature on earth.

Though not the longest mountain range - that distinction goes to the Andes of South America - it is easily the highest; averaging six thousand meters along its northern rampart and claiming all fourteen of the world's eight thousand meter peaks. The highest mountain in the Western Hemisphere, Argentina's Aconcagua (22,841ft/6962m) would not make the top two hundred in the Himalaya, where more than thirty mountains exceed twenty-five thousand feet! Aptly named, the abode of snow boats the world's largest subpolar glacial systems and the deepest land gorges. All that snow is the source of three of the world's great riverine systems - the Indus, the Ganges, and the Brahmaputra - and enfolds one sixth of the world's people in its watershed. If not for the Himalaya there would be no fertile soil on the Indo-Gangetic Plain, nor any life-affirming rain.

The Himalaya, simply put, gives life.

It can also facilitate death.

***

While there was still some light left in the sky and on the trail, William motioned for Ryder to stop hiking and come to a rest. William had been using gravity and the slippery snow to continue to pull Dave down the mountain while wrapped warmly in his sleeping bag. Dave rarely was awake and William was thankful for that. As much pain as William was in physically and emotionally he knew Dave was in even worse straights.

William took the mini-shovel out of his rucksack and started to carve out a snow cave from a mound of the white fluffy stuff that had fallen earlier and accumulated near a large rock. It looked like a safe place to spend the night before the temperatures dropped too far. After a couple of attempts to dig William knew his injuries would not let him complete the job. He handed the shovel over to his nephew and patiently explained the proper way to fashion out a snow cave from that blob of snow. It was hard work but Ryder welcomed it as a diversion from the reality of what had occurred. Ryder was happy to not see Nick's face in death's repose every time he closed his eyes.

Within an hour all three men were encamped inside Ryder's creation. As the wind howled outside they were warm and relatively comfortable. None of the three spoke for the longest time. Each thought the other two were asleep though none were. William looked over to his nephew and saw his eyes were scanning the ceiling of their snow cave with the little light that was left.

"We're lucky to be alive." William said to his nephew but it was Dave that chose to answer.

"I don't feel lucky."

William pivoted his head from Ryder to Dave and with sympathetic eyes replied, "I know," and he searched for more words but could only repeat himself, "I know."

After some time to reflect Dave then said, "I know what you mean, though, William. I do. I really do."

"How's your back feeling?" William asked his friend out of concern.

"Actually, much better, I think anyway." Dave's voice sounded brighter now. "I don't know if it's the cold, and it's frozen my pain away, or laying flat for so long while Ryder pulled me down the mountain," Dave chuckled and then continued, "but I don't really notice the pain. I'll try walking tomorrow."

"Yes, see how you feel." William said kindly.

"And Ryder, thanks for taking care of me and patching me up!" Dave said and Ryder lifted his head and turned to the man.

"Oh, don't thank me, it was my uncle who told me what to do. Without his -"

"What?" William asked, interrupting his nephew. "Told you what to do? What are you talking about?"

"On the mountain, you told me what to do to help Dave."

William shook his head. "I didn't. I really didn't. I didn't say one word to you the whole time. I was, I was…" William's voice drifted off as he didn't want to say Nick's name and bring attention back to that tragedy.

"Uncle, you did!" Ryder said while raising his head and his voice. He was adamant that his uncle instructed him.

William thought about it quietly and let the snow cave be silent save the wind that made its way through a series of small air slits. Each man was alone with his own thoughts. William finally spoke, "Third Man Factor."

Neither Ryder nor Dave spoke and asked the obvious question, what was a 'Third Man Factor'?

William knew what they were thinking and explained, "I had read a lot of this one expedition by this one British explorer up Everest back in the 1930s, Smyth was his name. He wrote of feeling accompanied by another explorer, who wasn't there. He thought, or rather felt like this other person was there, but no one was there with him. It's hard to explain. Or even to comprehend. And I've had a couple of buddies tell me when they were out on a mountain, and things got rough, there was a voice that spoke to them. Told them what to do. Saved their lives and yet, they were alone. Shackleton felt the same thing when he explored the Antarctic a couple of decades before that. I don't know, but that's kind of what it sounds like happened to you, Ryder."

Ryder let that sink in until his exhaustion, and the cold, overtook him and he fell asleep in the snow cave for a few precious hours.

***

Dave did not know why, but he felt no pain in his back when he woke up five hours later in the snow cave. He didn't feel much of his hands nor feet either and though that should have troubled him, it didn't.

As he started to walk behind William and in front of Ryder his steps were short, choppy, and awkward, but he was happy he was at least walking. William tried to talk him out of walking this morning but Dave would have none of it. William told Ryder to watch Dave closely and stay behind him at all times so his old buddy wouldn't slip and fall off of the mountain or into some deep crevasse, never to be seen again.

With gravity helping them the three began to make good time. The cold dulled not only Dave's back pain but also William's injuries. By the early afternoon they had made it sufficiently low enough on the mountain to spot their first yak train and farmer. The bells attached to the great beasts made a gentle tinkling sound that belied their enormous size and strength. William smiled and tried not to grimace as he waved and said, "Namaste" to the farmer who then returned the salutation. The encounter took no more than maybe a minute but it buoyed the spirits of the three men as they now thought they had a good chance of returning to civilization and safety.

It was at this point that the realization hit Dave the hardest. Now that he was no longer in a life and death struggle to survive, his mind went to his recently departed friend. Dave thought about how he would never see Nick's face again. Dave would never make him laugh and hear that unique laughter that Nick would bellow when feeling especially happy, which Dave could often make him feel.

Tears quietly streamed down Dave's face and eventually froze onto his cheeks as he trundled downward off that mountain. He made no noise, save a sniffle here and there. He did not want to draw attention to his misery and pain. He felt selfish with it. It was just his. Dave then thought about Nick's wife, and three year old daughter, and realized soon they would be sharing and exceeding his pain and misery over his friend's death.

Dave then looked over at William and an extra layer of sickness fell over him. The guilt that William must be feeling, Dave thought, must be insurmountable. It was Williams' idea, his plan, and his cajoling that made this trip take place. None of them in their right mind would have thought of this much less agreed to it unless William was so persistent and thorough in his presenting the idea to them.

And now the poor man will have to live with this, Dave thought. William's good intentions soured.

Dave then looked over at Ryder and was thankful and sort of happy again. He was happy that the young man didn't get seriously or permanently injured, or like Nick, worse. Dave could only see a few scratches on the teenager's temple but other than that he looked fine. He was glad Ryder was going home to his Leanne and all the teenage joy that meant. Dave was relieved and smiled as he lumbered down the snowy path. Yes, Ryder and Leanne could spend the rest of their lives together. And that's when Dave remembered he was going home to a home that no longer included him.

Sometimes injuries and scars don't always spout blood, bruise, break, or show on the surface.

***

CRESTED BUTTE, COLORADO
APRIL, 2019

When Mrs. Kravitz's husband became impotent she was at first mortified, then embarrassed for herself and then for him, and then she became empathetic and then eventually her number one emotion was thankfulness. Having never been one of her favorite chores, now that he was impotent she was relieved her duties in that department were over.

Once Mr. Kravtiz became impotent he got very crabby, and also very nosey. Since he now had extra time and energy, in between lashing out at his wife and friends as well as strangers, he now started a neighborhood watch program. Mr. Kravitz was excited to be excited about something again since he became…so he went out and bought a box of whistles and a plethora of yellow fluorescent vests. His first meeting attracted two visitors. His second just one. By the third meeting he was the leader as well as the sole follower. To be fair, his neighborhood was fairly safe and inviting and did not really cry out for a watch group. Organization and mobilizing were just two more talents that Mr. Kravitz lacked as he occupied his 60s. He returned the box of whistles and the trunk full of safety vests and partook the supremely important task of keeping his neighborhood safe in solitude.

Most days yielded no excitement and instead much disappointment. But this warm and sunny spring day brought to him the gift of a strange car to his neighborhood that deigned to park right in front of Mr. Kravitz house. As he stood up from his easy chair and grabbed his trusty pair of binoculars from their hanging place on a peg next to his jacket and hat, he made an audible sound of joy. It was such a loud sound of joy his wife in the next room wondered if he had tripped and hurt himself.

He sat back down in his chair and focused the binoculars on the car and its driver. His hands shook with excitement but he eventually was able to see who the driver was. A woman. A woman about forty years old or so. The windows were down. As her tattooed arm hung out of the driver's side window he also saw a plume of smoke exit the car. A few seconds later another one did. Mr. Kravitz was enthralled. Mrs. Kravitz hoped the car would stay awhile and thus occupy her husband for the rest of the afternoon.

***

Mrs. Kravitz got her wish. The car never moved for the next couple of hours. In fact, Mr. Kravitz was excited seeing a thin, mostly white and slightly tattooed arm languidly hanging out of the driver's side open window. Mr. Kravitz scrunched his nose at the sight. That was one thing, and maybe the only thing, he and his neighbor from across the street had in common, neither one liked tattoos, especially on girls. Mr. Kravitz did not know that his neighbor didn't like tattoos because they never talked. Mr. Kravitz, upon moving into the neighborhood, took an instant dislike to his slightly younger neighbor the first time he saw him cutting his grass shirtless and showing off his trim and muscular body. No, Mr. Kravitz did not like him after seeing that. Especially after hearing Mrs. Kravitz comment admiringly about his neighbor's shirtless torso.

It was late afternoon now and the girl was asleep. Mr. Kravitz kept his vigil going and his binoculars at the ready, just in case. Mrs. Kravitz enjoyed her freedom.

***

Valerie had hoped she would wake up when she heard his car engine drive by and park in his driveway but those sounds were not forthcoming and so she slept. It had been a long trip from Seattle so she closed her eyes and dozed, hoping she'd wake up to see him.

Singing loudly as he neared his neighborhood, Ryder quieted his singing a smidge as he entered the familiar street where he lived. He was the first house built on this block, by a full decade. When he moved in it was just forest and one dirt road. The sprawl of Crested Butte eventually engulfed his area and soon his property was bordered by many suburban houses that looked very different from the log cabin he helped build and lived in.

The soft clicky clicks sounds of his ten speed bicycle pedals while he coasted was not enough to wake up Valerie from her slumber in her rental car and so Ryder turned into his driveway unseen by anyone, except, of course, Mr. Kravitz, who saw everything as he sat impotently in his chair near the picture window of his house.

Ryder brought his bike inside his cabin, hung it up on the two poles high on his side wall, and then went back outside to get his mail. He looked up at the car that Valerie slept in but really gave it no mind. He deposited most of the mail into the garbage in his kitchen and then went back outside and checked on the rose bushes in his backyard.

Valerie finally woke up, yawned, and wanted to stretch her legs. Mr. Kravitz liked the look of her legs as she stood and moved them in various directions while her short shorts ran high on her thighs. He didn't like them enough to where certain body parts of his would start working again and Mrs. Kravitz's peace would soon be disturbed, but he admired Valerie's shapely legs just the same.

Valerie walked up to Ryder's driveway and hesitantly investigated closer to his cabin and couldn't help peaking into his kitchen window. She then peaked into the dining room window looking for signs of life and saw none. She stared intently at the decorations and any pictures on the walls or tables that she could see to help her understand a little better possibly who -

"Who are you?" A loud male voice rang in her ears and she was so startled that she jumped forward and bumped her nose on the glass in front of her.

"Ouch!" Valerie yelled, followed by a string of obscenities.

"What are you doing looking in my windows?" Ryder asked, louder this time as he walked closer to her.

Mr. Kravitz was having the afternoon of his life watching all of this play out from the comfort of his easy chair.

"Ouch!" Valerie said louder this time, hoping to elicit some sympathy but to no avail, Ryder's eyes were still crinkled in anger.

"Who are you?"

"Who are you?"

"You're on my property, who are you?" Ryder asked forcefully, a tension in his voice that usually didn't exist.

"I"m Valerie Brown."

The name meant nothing to Ryder. He continued to stare at her in a menacing way that made her continue.

"From Cleveland."

"Ohio?"

"Yes! Are you Ryder?"

"Maybe."

"Ryder Nowacki?"

"I said maybe."

"I've been waiting for you."

"I still don't know who you are."

"I told you. I'm Valerie Brown." There was no recognition, not that there should be, they had never met.

"Congrats, you're Valerie Brown. And I'm calling the police." Ryder said and started to walk into his house.

"Nick's daughter. Nick Brown." Valerie called out and hoped there would be a spark of recognition.

There was.

Ryder came right back out of the door and looked at her, from toes to nose. "Wait, Valerie Brown?"

"That's what I said!" Valerie put an extra emphasis on her words as a way to make Ryder feel guilty for doubting and treating her thusly.

Ryder did not feel either guilt or remorse. Instead he smiled and simply stated, "Why didn't you say so from the beginning?"

Mr. Kravitz was crestfallen seeing Ryder and the mystery girl disappear into the house with no further drama.

Valerie got right to the point and explained her whole plan to go back to Tibet and that mountain but then so did Ryder. "No."

"But you didn't even - " Valerie began to plead but Ryder cut her off again with a wave of his hand.

"I'm never going back there."

"But I have to. I have to see. I have to experience and say goodbye and get peace for myself."

"Go ahead, but do it without me." Ryder stated and then stood up and began to pace the room, almost looking for an escape.

"I can't!" Valerie protested, laying her soul exposed. "I can't do this without you. You're the only one that knows."

Ryder was about to ask but then he understood and wisely said nothing. He searched for something comforting to say but Valerie did not give him time.

"You're the only one who knows where my Daddy died. You're the only one left who knows where he's buried." Valerie's toughness melted away as her face betrayed any walls she thought she could construct.

"Valerie." Ryder said tenderly and with compassion.

"If I can face it, you can!" Valerie challenged and Ryder knew she was well within her bounds.

Ryder still was not giving up his defense, "The climb, the ascent, it's not for the inexperienced."

"I'm fit and -"

"It's technical and -"

"I'm no newbie, I've climbed a bunch of peaks."

"Yes, here in America, I'm guessing. Big difference." Ryder countered, still pacing and sensing his resolve weakening.

"Dude, I can -"

Ryder spied her vape pipe. "You ain't climbing anything, Valerie, until you can quit that thing!"

Valerie was confused at first until he pointed at and then grabbed it from where it was sticking out of her pocket.

"That?" Valerie asked in reference to what Ryder was now holding up high in a way of vindication.

"Yes, that. Altitude sickness will kill you out there if you're still sucking on that thing!" Ryder said righteously.

"I'm fit." Valerie declared and sat a bit more upright and puffed out her chest just a smidge.

"We'll see." Ryder said and instantly regretted his words. It meant if she passed a simple test then he would acquiesce. Valerie picked up on this and smiled and then stood up and put out her hand for Ryder to shake.

"If I pass we go?" Valerie excitedly asked.

"I never said that!"

"Yes, you basically did."

Ryder was trapped and cornered. He did the only thing he could, he quickly changed the subject, "How did you find me?"

"Not hard." Valerie said and mimicked typing into her phone and the wonders of google and the internet.

Ryder paused and regrouped. He then thought of a diversion and asked, "So, Val,why now?"

Valerie thought it was a good sign that he went from the proper 'Valerie' to the more casual 'Val'. "No time like the present." Valerie answered yet did not tell the whole story. She wasn't sure she ever would.

There was silence. Neither knew what to say to advance their cause. Ryder looked at the clock. Valerie spoke first.

"Why don't you have a car?"

"I have a bike." Ryder answered without really answering.

Valerie paused for a second but then replied, "Lots of people have both, you know, Ryder."

The way she said it made him begrudgingly laugh and then so did she, loudly and for a while.

"Why don't you have a cell phone?" Valerie then asked.

"How do you know I don't?"

"I texted a number and no reply, then checked it out and was told it was a landline. Who has a landline anymore?"

"Me."

"Me." Valerie repeated what Ryder said in a slightly mocking way. "So weird." Valerie said while rolling her eyes but keeping a slight smile on her face and Ryder simply shrugged. "You're a 'try hard'. You're trying too hard." Ryder looked at her blankly which she mistook for not understanding what she meant. "Trying hard to be different."

"You wish."

"I wish?"

"You wish. I am no 'try hard'. Not about that, anyway."

Valerie did not want this conversation to disintegrate into rancor, that would not help her cause in the least. It was her that now needed to regroup and she held up her right index finger and said, "I have to get something out of my car to show you, I'll be right back!" Valerie left and was back in under a minute. Ryder barely had time to think of what to do or say in the brief time it took her to return from her parked rental car.

"I have these maps, and these -"

Ryder cut her off, "I don't need to see any maps. I don't want to see any maps." There was no anger or malice in his voice, Ryder stated it matter of factly.

Valerie panicked and went to her next weapon of persuasion quicker than she planned on, "I can pay you handsomely!"

Ryder smiled, looked around his modest cabin and then looked back at her, "Do you think money motivates me?"

Valerie laughed and the tension in the room evaporated. "Yeah, I guess not. But still, I can and will pay you handsomely."

"Want to sit?" Ryder asked, hoping if maybe they weren't standing the conversation would go to another venue.

Valerie shook her head 'no', "I'm too worked up."

Ryder shrugged his shoulders, looked resigned to his fate, and sat down and listened to her plea. "Obviously."

"I looked into what a normal guiding company would cost and I will double it! More than double it!" Valerie added when Ryder's reaction did not equal what she thought it would. "I can pay you fifty thousand dollars, cash, under the table, no taxes taken out!"

Ryder's eyes did widen and despite his best efforts his countenance betrayed him. He was ashamed of himself for letting money sway his resolve. Ryder equated having money with freedom but he also equated the pursuit of money as the antithesis of freedom. All his bills were covered but this windfall would give him much more freedom.

Valerie saw she had turned the conversation and there was now a glimmer of hope that her dream just might happen. She thought it best to retreat and ingratiate herself to him in a way he would appreciate. "That drive, my legs… want to hike around your forest here and you could show me around?"

Ryder looked at the clock on the wall and deduced that he had a little time for a possible hike. "Yes, we could. I have a couple of friends coming by later." Valerie could not get a read on Ryder yet, was he annoyed or even angry she was there or was he fine or maybe even happy with it?

Valerie made it a point to keep smiling and stay positive, "Great, I'll change into my hiking shoes."

Valerie walked over to her suitcase and opened it, retrieved her shoes and it was then that Ryder even noticed it was there on the floor next to the door. "Are you staying here? In my cabin?"

Butterflies circled her stomach upon hearing him ask her that. Before she could muster the courage to answer Ryder asked another question, "And for how long?" Ryder's last question put her at ease, like her staying was a fact accompli.

"Only if it's no trouble." Valerie knew what to say next, "I just have so many questions about my Dad I'd love to ask her you."

That sentence had the desired effect on Ryder. "Sure, sure" he stammered and then regained his control, "no trouble at all. I'd love to be able to tell you all that I can remember about your father."

But it was a 'trouble' to Ryder. He really enjoyed his privacy. He was extremely social, but only up to a point and never with the thought of someone staying with him. Or by the size of Val's suitcase, possibly living with him, for days upon days. Maybe even weeks. No, Ryder did not like this at all. But she was Nick Brown's daughter. That counted for a lot. It defeated any resistance he might offer up.

As Valerie walked back into the living room while holding her shoes she looked at the framed picture on the wall. It was taken back in 1982. In the picture was her youthful and handsome father holding Dolma, the three year old Tibetan little girl he had played with that fell asleep in his lap. "My dad." Valerie said quietly as Ryder walked up behind her and looked closely at the picture.

"What a night that was."

"I'd love to hear all about it." Valerie said and sat down and put on her shoes.

"We'll walk and talk." Ryder promised.

Valerie laced up her shoes and they were out the door and into the peaceful bliss of the forest within a minute.

Mr. Kravitz perked up from his chair and put his binoculars immediately up to his eyes upon seeing Valerie and Ryder exit his cabin. The old voyeur was quickly disappointed as the two turned a corner and disappeared from his view into the forest behind Ryder's cabin. Mr. Kravitz stood up, went to the bathroom, then took a bag of cheese doodles from the kitchen and placed them on top of his binoculars on the table next to his chair. He vowed to be ready when they returned.

***

CRESTED BUTTE
MAY,1861

The two Ute Indian scouts were alert but relaxed as they sat astride their mustangs on that mountain and surveyed the vast, beautiful, and more importantly, empty wilderness in front of them that late morning. The Ute people had been in North America since the end of the last Ice Age and had taken to the western states especially well once they encountered that beautiful and fast animal. The Ute Indians had been riding that type of Spanish horse, the mustang, since they had fled from those Europeans in what would later be called New Mexico two hundred years before. The mustangs greatly benefitted the Ute tribe because they were so hardy, adaptable, and well-suited to the harsh conditions of the American West. The mustangs allowed the Ute Indians to hunt buffalo more effectively, travel great distances, and raid other groups for resources.

The Ute Indians were a fierce and powerful tribe thanks to their horsemanship. One of the resources they raided other communities for was slaves, which they then sold to get more horses. One female slave was worth the equivalent of eight horses.

The two Ute scouts that scanned the horizon that clear and warm morning had been trained to ride a horse from the very first moments that they could walk. They also learned at a very early age how to take care and feed not just one horse but an entire herd.

Suddenly the morning was not so placid anymore as they spotted a speck of movement several miles below in the valley. The scouts were worried as the travellers were headed west from east. That could mean only one thing, a column of white settlers, possibly an army detachment.

The two scouts used their skills of horsemanship and subterfuge over the course of the next few hours and were able to make their way closer and closer to the interlopers while never being detected. They squinted and then dismounted from their mustangs and crept even closer still.

What they saw were indeed white men, but thankfully for the Indians these were not soldiers. The scouts hid silently and kept watching the men as they slowly invaded their territory. The white men had shovels and other metal equipment instead of rifles. These men were an advancing party of placer miners.

While many placer miners were famously panning and sluicing for gold in California and silver in Virginia City, these men would eventually discover a different treasure, coal.

Before the decade was over the Ute's signed a treaty that led to the creation of a reservation that covered the western half of Colorado and encompassed fifty-six million acres. A couple of years later, in 1873, Ferdinand V. Hayden was ambling throughout the Elk Mountains and summited Teocalli Mountain on a surveying expedition when he looked out on the same vista of snow capped mountains that those two Ute Indian scouts had and declared, "Those are the crested buttes".

The town now had a name even before it was actually a town. Howard F. Smith took care of that detail five years later in 1878 when he laid out the town and also built a smelter and a sawmill to service all of the mining camps in the surrounding mountains. Smith became the town's first mayor and then its benefactor when he was able to persuade the railroad to go through Crested Butte which ended the town's isolation. In just a couple of years the town's population tripled and over the next few decades tripled again as the coal industry thrived and Crested Butte with it.

***

Though the temperatures were tepid, maybe getting as high as the mid fifties, Valerie was drenched in sweat and her breathing was loud and hoarse enough to cause birds a hill away to fly off. Everytime they gained enough altitude so that Ryder started to feel a bead of perspiration on his forehead, Valerie would stop and lean against a tree and could barely catch her breath.

After the third time this happened Ryder asked her point blank, "Do you really think you can climb Minya Konka when you're struggling this epically up this measly little hill in my backyard?"

The burning in her throat and lungs kept Valerie from answering Ryder back. Well, that and it was the truth.

And the fourth time she stopped and leaned against a tree and then, against her better judgement, she took out her vape and took a long drag and then let the smoke circle the branches above, Ryder shook his head in disgust.

"Are you serious about trying to climb Minya Konka?" Ryder did not ask it to mock or insult her, he sincerely wanted to gauge her level of commitment. He stepped closer and looked into her exhausted eyes.

She didn't answer with words, she couldn't, but she nodded her head while wiping more sweat from her brow.

Ryder stepped even closer and took the vape from her hand and threw it high and far into the forest greenery. There was silence for a moment as she couldn't believe he did that and he waited for the severity of her reaction. He didn't intend to do that, but the whole stupidity of it all overwhelmed him.

"That was a dick move!" Valerie shouted at him and then instantly regretted the vocal exertion on her burning throat. To her surprise, Ryder calmly and slowly turned away and looked off into the distance of the seemingly endless hills.

Valerie did not know this, but Ryder had been deliberating on the question of whether or not he would guide her to that deadly mountain in Tibet. Though he had rejected the idea initially when she asked, since then he had been really contemplating on whether or not he should do it for her.

With every step they took up the hill Ryder was debating the pros and cons of undertaking such an excursion. Ryder wasn't sure he could face the place where so many terrible things happened. He countered that with the idea that maybe that is precisely what he should do, face it head on.

***

Mrs. Kravitz could hear the old, rusted springs coil and uncoil in the easy chair that often housed her husband, even from the parlor room where she read her true crime books in between phone calls with her two sisters. She could tell by the speed of the sounds if he was excited and active in the chair or not. Right now he sounded very active. But instead of peeking into the living room where he was perched in front of the huge bay window to look at him, and thus maybe have to interact with him, she went to the parlor window and looked to see what caused him to be in such a stir.

Two people were riding up to Ryder's house on bikes. One was a young man in his early twenties and the other appeared to be a woman in her fifties, with wild and wavy light colored hair and an equally flowing wild and wavy and multi-colored summer dress. Mrs. Karvitz surmised it was the woman in all her eccentric glory that had so tickled her husband's fancy at that moment. She watched the two get off of their bicycles, lean them against Ryder's garage, and then walk into his house.

Mrs. Kravitz then heard no more springs in the chair coil or uncoil for the rest of the afternoon.

***

"Not Cheap Trick again!" Mesa, the woman of the wild and wavy hair and summer dress fame, pleaded as Ryder put on music. The four had been talking and munching on tortilla chips for the past hour. Ryder and Valerie had just returned from their hike within a minute of Mesa and the young man riding over.

"All this talking about our glory days in the 80's, I have to listen to my go to 80's group! Cheap Trick!" Ryder answered while squirting more ketchup onto his plate which he then dipped his chips into.

"I just can't get used to that!" Mesa said while watching Ryder do that. "Ketchup and tortilla chips." Mesa added in disgust.

"Hey! You put ketchup on french fries don't you?"

"I don't eat french fries." Mesa countered.

"Oh, Miss Vegan Healthy Non-processed Organic woman!" Ryder said in a heavy mocking tone.

Mesa smiled and did not seem fazed by his comments in the least. She wore it as a badge of pride. Mesa was never fazed by anything Ryder had to say, she had known him from way, way back. They went to high school together. She, in fact, was the object of his fascination before even Leanne. Mesa did not know much about him back then, he was just another pesky boy buzzing around that she swatted away along with many others. They just happened to cross paths randomly decades later when she fell off the ski lift one day in Crested Butte and lamented, "What's a surfer girl doing trying to ski?"

To which Ryder, standing there on the mountain and laughing at her asked, "Surfer girl? Where are you from?"

"Lots of places." Mesa answered, "South America, California, Florida -"

"Where in Florida?"

"Clearwater."

"I grew up in Clearwater!"

"No way! I went to Clearwater Central Catholic High School."

"No way! I got kicked out of Clearwater Central Catholic!" Ryder shot back, honestly, and a friendship that normally would not have happened was born.

Valerie decided to change the subject, "Why do you call him John," Val asked, pointing first to Mesa and then the young man, "but you call him Sven?" and then pointing to Ryder and back to the young man again.

"Because Ryder is weird." Mesa answered and Ryder did his best to try to pretend to look hurt.

"He looks like a 'Sven', doesn't he?" Ryder asked Valerie. "See those Nordic features and dimples?"

Valerie looked at John/Sven and conceded, "Yes, I guess so. Kind of. Are you from Nordic stock?" Valerie asked John/Sven.

"I'm Italian." John/Sven answered and those were half the words he had spoken since arriving. He was an immense man of few words. He stood well over six feet tall and had what appeared to be legs coming out of his shoulders instead of arms. Rare was a day he wasn't in the gym.

Valerie looked around Ryder's cabin and then asked him, "Why don't you have a dog? You look like the type of dude that would have a dog. Seems like this place would be perfect for one."

"That's what we've been telling him, Valerie, to get a dog." John/Sven answered and then looked at Ryder.

"Oh, just call me Val, Valerie is too long a name." Val said to John/Sven and the others and then also looked at Ryder.

"I told you guys before." Ryder pleaded, though Val hadn't a clue what he meant. She looked first to Mesa and then John/Sven for an answer. Ryder finally explained, "I had a dog, a perfect dog, she was my best friend. She loved to hike, swim, and drink beers by the bonfire with me."

Val raised her eyebrows at Ryder.

"Well, I drank beers and she watched me by the bonfire. But she died. I just can't face getting another dog. It'll never be as great as my first. Never be as loving. Never be the same. I just can't."

There was an uncomfortable silence after Ryder left himself so open and vulnerable to them.

Val took it upon herself to change the subject. "How did you all meet?" Val asked as they took their drinks and chips, and Ryder took his plate of ketchup out into the backyard to enjoy the evening's sunset in the cool upper elevation air.

"They work where I work." Ryder answered.

"You two also guide in the mountains?" Val asked while finishing her second glass of white wine.

John/Sven shook his head and Mesa smiled and said simply, "No."

"At the supermarket." Ryder stated. "Mountain Air Organic Grocer."

"Wait, you shop there and met?" Val asked, confused.

"No, we all work there." Ryder explained. "I've been working there for years and years, then Mesa joined up a couple of years ago and then just last year we talked Sven into working there too!"

"Really?" Val said thoughtfully, trying to process this latest bit of news into Ryder Nowacki.

Ryder could see the look on Val's face but he didn't feel the need to explain himself. He decided to let her think what she wanted to think.

She did. Val thought to herself, "If he is so poor that he's working at a supermarket at his age then…"

The night continued in a convivial fashion as more wine was drunk, more chips were eaten, sunsets were watched and enjoyed, and take out dinner was ordered. At one point John/Sven and Ryder were sitting by the roaring bonfire emptying a couple more beers when John/Sven looked around to make sure they couldn't be overheard and then asked Ryder, "So, are you interested in Valerie?"

Ryder now looked around to make sure it really was just him and John/Sven within earshot of the bonfire and then answered, "No, not like that! No! Not at all. Wait, why do you ask?"

"She's pretty, a bunch of years younger than you, nice bod, seems funny, seems friendly."

"No, not my type. She looks like she's 42 trying to look like she's 22 from 1982." Ryder quipped and then looked pleased with himself.

His reference was completely lost on John, Sven. "Wait, what?"

"Back in 1982, it seemed every girl wanted to look like Joan Jett, or Pat Benatar. That short spikey hair look. That's just not my type." Ryder said this and thought back on who exactly was his type, to a tee. John/Sven did not know who those two girls that Ryder mentioned were or what they looked like. "Google them on your magic rectangle. Look up Joan Jett and Pat Benatar, but make sure it's from 1982. You'll see what I mean."John/Sven did as Ryder continued, "That, plus the tattoos and the vaping and, I don't know. I like my girls to be girls. I'm not into harsh."

John/Sven found the images and laughed loudly. Ryder thought John/Sven was a good laugher and because of that, and his young friend being such a good audience, he liked to make him laugh often.

"Oh yeah, wow, I see what you mean. Yes, that's a no thank you for me either, I like girls with longer hair than me."

Now it was Ryder's turn to laugh loudly.

Before midnight Mesa and John/Sven rode off, a smidge wobbly, on their bikes and Val still was not sure if they were a couple. Or was Mesa after Ryder? Val hadn't a clue as Ryder showed no interest in Mesa, Nor did Val perceive that Ryder had an interest in her either. Not that that was her plan, to seduce him to get him to take her up that far away mountain but it probably wouldn't hurt her cause.

As Ryder fixed up the one spare room for her to sleep in, Val finished cleaning up the kitchen. She wondered if he would try to kiss her, or anything else. She wasn't sure how she would react if he did.

"What did you think about my two friends?" Ryder asked while he readied Val's room for her.

Val wasn't sure if she wanted to be honest. She liked John/Sven and thought him to be friendly if not a bit too quiet. But she was pretty sure she wasn't going to be best friends with Mesa. Val wondered if there was too much unspoken competition between them. "I liked John, or Sven, or whatever you call him." Val answered and then was quiet as she was trying to choose her words carefully.

"But Mesa not so much?" Ryder asked.

"No, she's ok." Val replied but without much conviction.

Ryder poked his head out of the spare bedroom and asked Val, "What was it? The flowing hair? The flowing dress? Her flowing way about her? She does make an entrance, does she not? Can't forget that lady!" Ryder said in an admiring way.

"It's just that, I told her that I was once in South America, Columbia, one of the places she's from. And I told her how I had talked down a street vendor on this one necklace from like twenty bucks to two dollars and she said back to me, 'Oh, I would never try to cheat a poor person.' Like, what?"

"She's just a very caring and empathetic person. I think you just took it wrong. She's really kind, and has been through a lot."

"I don't know, she just seems like a 'look at me' kind of person. How she dresses, talks, everything screams 'look at me'!"

"I think if you got to know her, really knew her, you'd see her gifts are deep and genuine." Ryder said and then finished his task.

Once the last dish was put away she walked over to the spare bedroom just as Ryder was walking out of it and he stopped in front of her. Val stared at him, into his deep blue eyes, and thought that maybe, yes, she would -

"It might get cold tonight but I only have one electric blanket, did you want it?" Ryder asked as she stared and then successfully re-grouped.

"One?"

"Or will the two comforters be enough?"

"Sure, they'll be fine."

Ryder smiled and patted the top of her head as if she was a child or a family pet, and then went into his bedroom and shut the door. Val stood for a moment, gathered her wits about her, and then went into her bedroom and also closed the door. It took her quite a few tosses and turns and blanket reconfiguring to finally fall asleep.

***

The next morning Ryder woke up before the rising sun and instead of laying in his bed to do a half an hour of deep breathing exercises, he immediately got up and quietly made himself some green tea with honey. He was careful to silently pad about his house because he did not want Val to wake up. And not out of consideration to her, but because he did not want to interact with her, or anyone else. After last night, with Mesa and John/Sven and Val, his social battery was empty.

Ryder felt that was one of the biggest differences between pre-Tibet Ryder and post-Tibet Ryder, his tolerance for excessive social interaction. A little conversation here and there, nothing deep, keep it light, and he was fine. Maybe even, once in a while, a deep conversation, to a point. Any more than that and he would check out.

Once his tea was done there was enough sunlight now that he didn't need his head lamp to go out into the forest. He dressed light and took just a coconut protein bar with him. He stealthily clicked his front door closed and escaped into the solitude of the surrounding hills.

***

The two hour time difference between Cleveland and Crested Butte meant that her body thought it was seven in the morning when in fact it was only five am for Val. She laid in bed and tried to fall back but just couldn't. She heard the ding of the microwave, she heard a faint gush of running water, she heard a gentle click of the front door. And then she heard nothing else as she continued to not sleep in that surprisingly comfortable bed that Ryder Nowacki had considerately prepared for her. Less than twenty-four hours ago he had never met her and now she was sleeping in his cabin and partaking of his hospitality. But will he be her guide to Tibet? That question gnawed at her and kept her from falling back to sleep.

Val got up and started to walk towards her purse and was about to reach into it when she stopped, swore out loud, and then turned back to bed. She had just remembered that Ryder had thrown her jewel pipe far into the great forestry unknown. Val continued to appraise Ryder's action as a 'dick move'.

She then left her bedroom and went to the kitchen window and saw it was a gorgeous morning with the sun streaming through the trees and decided to change her mood around. Val opened the refrigerator and looked for something to either eat or drink that would be healthy and make her feel clean. There was fresh squeezed orange juice and some raspberries courtesy of the organic market where Ryder and his friends worked. Val poured herself a glass of juice and began to pick at the raspberries while scrolling through her messages on her phone. Looking eagerly for something to interest her, but her phone disappointed her once again and none of the fleeting diversions proved to last.

Upon finishing her juice and most of the raspberries, Val cleaned up after herself in the kitchen and then began to look at the maps she brought of Tibet and its imposing and lethal mountains.

***

Mesa rolled, stretched her arms out wide, smiled, and then spread her legs out wide, all before opening her eyes as she lay in bed while a sunbeam splashed over her. Her long, maroon kashmir nightshirt absorbed the sun's warmth into her skin and she felt fully alive and fabulous, and she had only been awake for a couple of minutes. Her hands roamed her skin and she caressed the new day into her being. Her breathing became very deliberate and deeply full.

With her eyes still closed and a smile still on her face, she reached over to her night stand where she knew her prayer beads, also known as a mala, were waiting for her. She whispered her mantra intentionally to internalize the energetic harmony of the words and to raise her vibration. Mesa needed this time to start her day, every day. This routine was her formula to heal her body, protect her mind, and to manifest her desires for the day. It was the source of her strength.

Mesa took her time. To rush would be to fail. Her mantra was not just a sound, it was something that she strove to become.

Her past was littered with men who could not or would not understand and let her take her time.

Mesa interrupted her morning wake up routine to stand slowly and quietly and exited her bedroom. She lightly walked on her wooden floor past the guest bedroom where through the open door Mesa could see John's/Sven's hulking, sleeping form lay unclothed under a lone sheet. She smiled at the remembrance of the previous night's festivities and got herself a large glass of tepid water. She went back to her bedroom, careful not to wake him up. She was not concerned for his sleep, Mesa just did not want to be disturbed in her rituals. They were too important to her to be altered by another. She delicately closed her door, drank deeply, and lay back down on her solitary bed.

***

Val wasn't sure what to do with herself now that she had eaten, brushed her teeth, and finished most of her other morning time rituals. She was kind of bored. Ryder had a television but she hadn't a clue how to turn it or, or where a remote might be. His wi-fi was spotty at best so there wasn't much reception for her phone. Val decided to wander outside.

Upon opening the door she hesitated for a moment and wondered whether she should put a little more clothing on. A tank top and shorts without nothing underneath was all she had on, not even sandals, but she figured no one was awake and watching at that hour so she walked outside.

***

Mr. Kravitz shifted excitedly in his living room chair as he used his two hands to focus his binoculars on the scantily clad and shapely woman who was stretching provocatively in his neighbor's driveway across the street.

***

Val looked up at the large garage/barn type structure next to Ryder's drive-way. She hadn't really noticed it before, nor the hand painted sign that hung over the two large sliding barn doors that read "Krammit Inn". It took her a moment to get the joke but when she did she laughed out loud.

It was a pretty barn as far as barns go, she thought. A nice red color with tight trims of white on the borders. It took her two tries to get the door to budge but once it did it slid nicely open.

Once her eyes adjusted from the daylight to the darkness inside Val was amazed at what she saw. Right in front of her face was a thick rope hanging high from the rafters twenty-five feet up. There was also a huge truck tire lying to her left with a sledge hammer leaning against it. Various kettle bell weights and medicine balls were also in evidence. What she thought would house a bunch of rusty old trucks or other sorts of junk instead was a bastion of adventure type workout devices.

Val rubbed her hands together and wanted to test herself. Val grabbed the rope and looked to succeed. She failed. No matter how determined she was she could not climb up the rope, not even two hand lengths. She soon broke the skin on her palm and had to stop with much aggravation and embarrassment brewing inside her.

She left the barn and closed the two huge barn doors loudly as she looked around for any sign of Ryder. When she found none, she looked across the street at Mr. Kravitz window which caused him to drop his binoculars while he was ducking down quickly. Val never saw him spying on her, the sun's glare off of his picture window prevented it. Val went back into Ryder's cabin and shut the door with extra force. She again rued him throwing away her vaping pen into the wilderness.

***

Ryder knew he made the correct choice. The more he sweated and strained up the mountain the better he felt. The more his leg muscles ached the less his brain did. He talked, sometimes silently sometimes not, with himself about a variety of subjects, paramount being whether or not he should guide Val in Tibet. Both answers on the subject seemed justified and defensible.

He also wondered just how long she planned on staying with him. He didn't want to seem rude or unhospitable, but he never did invite her to begin with. Ryder liked his solitude, it was essential to him.

In between wrestling with those questions his mind would rewind to various losses, some huge and permanent, some just annoying. Some losses that were his fault, some that he had no say in. Ryder wasn't sure which of those two were the hardest to deal with. Ryder reasoned it was just better not to deal with any of those losses and he used the mountain climbing as a shovel to bury those feelings and problems deep away.

When he finally stopped to eat his protein bar he was in a much better mood and felt more like himself, whoever that was. Ryder felt like there were many different 'Ryders' day to day and what scared him was how little control he felt he had over which one would show up. His mind often drifted back to when he returned from Tibet in 1982 after the tragedy, and how his dark moods would overtake him without warning. He lamented those who got caught in the cross-fire. He thought about her. He thought about how he lost her. He wondered if there was a way to even out the bad karma of losing her. He logically knew he couldn't go back in time but could he possibly do something good now that would…and then he stopped himself. Ryder knew enough that when his mind began to fixate on his past with Leanne that he needed to redirect and so he got up and began to descend down the mountain at twice the pace he normally would, safety be damned!

***

John/Sven was in a predicament. It was a dilemma that happened every time he slept over at Mesa's place after an enjoyable night. He never quite knew what was expected of him the next morning. What complicated things is that they would see each other later at work. It could never be a hit and run though nor could it ever be the start of a lifelong love affair due to the age difference and what each was looking for. He wanted to be a gentleman, a good man, a good friend. He also wanted to leave.

John/Sven heard Mesa walking around and then returning to her room. He heard the bed move, the sheets being rearranged, and the glass returning to its night stand. Should he go in and say good morning to her, or go in and make it a good morning for her? Or should he just let himself out? He sighed and tried to think what the best option would be.

There was for sure, he reasoned, a thin line between Saturday night and Sunday morning.

***

Ryder was greeted with a big smile from Val when he came back home to his cozy cabin.

"Where were you?" Val asked, hoping Ryder would notice how much cleaning and tidying she did in his absence. She wanted to make herself useful and be a welcomed guest, and someone he would want to help.

"I went hiking up Randy Mountain." Ryder stated, taking off his boots and laying them on the mat near the kitchen door.

"Oh, so that's what that mountain is called."

"No, actually it isn't. I honestly don't even know if it has a name. And to be honest, I don't even know if it's technically a mountain. Might just be a big hill for I know." Ryder explained and got himself a small glass, filled it with water, drank it, and then repeated the process another seven times.

"Wait, then why do you call it Randy Mountain?"

"Do you really want to know?" Ryder asked with a sly, mischievous smile.

Val smiled back.

"Yes!"

"Well, shortly after I moved here…wait, do you really, are you sure you really want to hear this story?"

"Of course!" Val exclaimed, getting more interested by the second.

"Well, when I first moved here I didn't know too many people. Actually I didn't know anybody. But I went hiking up that mountain, or hill, whatever you want to call it, and I met this really attractive girl that was also solo hiking. I stopped, we talked, we hit it off, and then when I offered for her to come down to my cabin to hang out, just hang out mind you!" Ryder stressed earnestly.

"Sure," Val teased back, disbelieving, "just hang out."

"She took me to where she had set up her camp, and her tent. And then, and then," Ryder paused. "Well. It sure was a nice tent." Ryder sheepishly laughed and drank another glass of water.

Val looked at him, laughed along with him, and thought he was a pretty charming slightly older fellow. Then she understood, "Oh, Randy, I get it now. I thought you were going to say her name was Randi."

"Dear heavens."

***

Mr. Kravitz was disappointed with the lack of viewable opportunities that Ryder and Val presented him that day. Anytime he got up to either use the restroom or get more snacks he made it a point to be extra efficient and quick. He'd rush back to his chair and place his trust binoculars up to his eyes and scan Ryder's driveway, then front yard, then part of the backyard he could see. Always there was nothing, but empty vistas of inactivity. He clenched the binoculars harder in misguided hopes that would cause Ryder and Val to somehow come out and be observed.

"Honey, I'm going to the store." Mrs. Kravtiz said, grabbing her purse. "Want anything special?"

"No, no, I'm fine."

"Want to come with me?" Mrs. Kravitz asked, not really wanting him to say 'yes' but feeling like she should offer.

"Maybe next time."

"Ok."

"Here." Mr. Kravitz said and did not quite stand but lifted himself a little bit and kissed her on the cheek.

"Enjoy your" slight pause "day."

***

Ryder could not shake his unsettled feeling. He could not out work his stressed demeanor. First he began to scrub the floors, and Val offered to help him, but it really wasn't a two person job so he rebuffed her. "I was going to cut the grass, you can do that, but only if you really want to."

"Sure." Val answered, trying to muster up enthusiasm. She never was one for grass cutting or other chores.

After Ryder got the grass cutter out of the storage area of the Krammit Inn and started it up for Val, he was now again alone in his thoughts. Scrubbing and thinking. Did he really want to take Val to Tibet and that mountain that killed her father? Even if he did, could she even handle the hiking and climbing, or the altitude?

Then he thought of Nick and the kindness Nick always showed him, and he knew he owed it to him. Both answers, yes and no, made sense and could be defended without hesitation. Ryder thought he could especially defend the decision of not taking and guiding Val in Tibet. In no way did it make sense or was realistic or feasible, not with her lack of mountaineering experience or physical fitness.

Yet, the more he scrubbed the floors the more the inconvenient answer kept slapping him in the face, he should take Val to that deadly mountain in Tibet in honor of her father and his friend, Nick. But there had to be caveats and conditions before he would agree to take and guide her.

As he worked up a sweat making his floors look shiny and clean he dismissed how troubled he still felt about it all and instead focused on the fact that at least he now had a solution.

***

After first stopping at the bank, Mrs. Kravitz then went to the food store where Ryder, Mesa, and John/Sven worked, though none of them were there at the time. After getting some cheese, crackers, and a bottle of wine she then walked back to her car and sat in it and stared out of the window. She put the key in the ignition and then starred some more out of the window but at nothing in particular while still not turning the key to start her car. A smile then crept onto her lips and she took a full, deep breath. Mrs. Kravitz then turned the key and her car started and she put it into drive and pulled out of the store parking lot.

After sending a text, she turned the corner and as she pulled into the driveway the garage door opened and she slowly parked her car into it. The door closed as soon as her foot was off the brake. She grabbed her bag of goodies that she had just purchased and walked through the garage door and into the kitchen area where she kicked off her shoes and was met with a tight hug and a deep kiss.

Theodore, or Teddy as she liked to call him, then led her into his bedroom where they snuggled on the bed and talked, occasionally kissed, and sometimes just lay contentedly for a good hour before anything else took place.

Mrs. Kravitz knew she had plenty of time before she had to head back home to her impoten, voyeuristic husband.

***

"Wait, so I have to pass some kind of physical fitness test?" Val asked as the sweat continued to pour down her forehead and into her eyes. The grass cutting took more out of her than she thought it would have. Ryder had given her what he thought was good news, that he would indeed guide her in Tibet, but first she had to prove she could physically make it. Val's initial reaction was of being insulted.

"It's not an easy climb, and the thin air can really do a number on you, I just have to be sure." Ryder explained as patiently as he could.

Val thought if she ever heard Ryder agree to this trip she would have been happy, but instead she snapped, "I'm not a child! I know what I can or cannot do, I sure don't need you to tell me!"

"That's where you're wrong." Ryder again tried to patiently explain. He then went into the various dangers that were lurking at such high altitude in Tibet and with such unpredictable terrain.

Val tried to make herself calm down but she found herself still worked up. Ryder went over the workout regime he wanted her to undertake, and also the breathing exercises and cold water immersion techniques that he found very useful in times of duress. Some his Uncle William had taught him four decades past along with Val's father. "Your Uncle William got my Dad to do this?" Val asked as Ryder demonstrated some of the offbeat meditative breathing methods.

"Oh, your Dad made a ton of fun of my Uncle William when he showed him, but he did try it."

"Really?" Val asked and Ryder nodded. "Because from what my Mom told me about my Dad - "

"I know, he was more than a smidge cynical and loved to make fun of everything. And everybody. Especially anything my Uncle William said, that's the kind of best friends they were." Ryder was smiling now, remembering.

"So my dad was a funny guy?"

Ryder beamed and answered, "Whoa, yes, so funny, even when I didn't get the jokes or understand exactly what he was talking about. Like this one night we were sitting around the bonfire and Dave starts to tell all these racist jokes and -"

Val looked mortified and Ryder saw this and wanted to assuage her concerns.

"No, no, it was the 80's, everybody was more laid back and joked about everything. Dave and your dad were making fun of every race you can think of. Hilarious jokes. Again, I didn't understand them all then but I just about peed my pants laughing at their delivery and the way they'd tell them. And then they started to do all these religious jokes, first the Catholics, then the Jews, then the Muslims, oh, it was 'hell- arious'! Seriously funny! They must have gone on for half an hour!"

Val wasn't so sure on how hilarious that particular bonfire must have been, but she was pleased that Ryder appreciated her father.

"No," Ryder added softly, "your dad was a really special person, right up until the end, we had such amazing times."

"I wish I could have been there, with all of you guys. Except for that last part."" Val said softly.

"What, the racist jokes?" Ryder sincerely wondered.

"No, well maybe yes, but no, when he died."

They had been standing in his kitchen but now she sat down on the chair that was next to the simple four person kitchen table.

Ryder reached down and put his hand on her shoulder as she sat there and looked at him plaintively. “I know.” A tear escaped from her eyes and dropped down onto his hand that rested comfortingly on her shoulder.

“So when do we start this workout torture routine?” Val asked while sitting upright, trying to sound upbeat, and quickly wiping her eyes with her hands.

“We can start tomorrow if you like.” Ryder answered, still keeping a tenderness to his voice.

“How about today?”

“After lunch?”

“Sounds great!” Val exclaimed and began to get very happy that her dream just might come to fruition.

***

“Were the stores crowded?” Mr. Kravitz asked from his chair as he heard his wife come home and put down some bags on their kitchen counter. He had a jackpot of an afternoon as Ryder and that new girl went into Ryder’s barn and left the two big doors open. Mr. Kravitz could watch them the whole time.

Mr. Kravitz was particularly pleased with the workout attire that Val had on, a sports bra and yoga shorts were all that covered her while she strenuously lifted weights and contorted her body in a series of highly challenging, and in Mr. Kravitz opinion, highly exciting poses and stances.

“Yes, very. Very crowded.” Mrs. Kravtiz answered and for a brief moment felt a twinge of guilt.

Mr. Kravitz looked at his watch and noticed the time, “Whoa, I guess they were. It’s almost dinner time.”

Mrs. Kravitz thought it was amazing, or was the word disturbing, how much time her husband spent watching other people live their lives. Any trace of guilt she harbored instantly evaporated.

"I'll start to get supper ready."

"Thank you, honey!" Mr. Kravitz said brightly, though he never lowered the binoculars from his eyes.

***

John/Sven began to giggle uncontrollably which caused him to have even more trouble catching his breath. Mesa slapped his chest and also giggled, "What's so funny, big boy, did you lay on a feather?"

"I just don't think I can get the hang of this tantric thing."

"You're just new at it, and young. But you're in good hands, I'll be patient and teach you." Mesa purred and John/Sven immediately knew she was true to her word. They both rather enjoyed their afternoons away from the organic market.

***

"It's cleansing, isn't it?" Ryder asked Val as her chest was heaving and she held a towel to her brow.

"I'm disgusting!" Val replied. She meant in appearance and also in stench, she could smell herself and it wasn't pretty.

"You're transforming."

"That's a polite word for what I am!" Val said and laughed at her own joke, and Ryder did too.

"First step. You did great."

"I'm so sore."

"You're really going to hate me tomorrow, today is nothing for soreness, it's always the next day that's worse."

"Oh great!"

"Are you going to shower now?"

"Don't you think I should?"

"For sure!" Ryder said and held his nose and she threw her towel at him. They both laughed again.

"Brat!"

"Remember, cold water. Ice cold water. For as long as you can, at least a minute in the shower."

"We'll see."

"I'm not asking."

"We'll see."

***

Mr. Kravitz missed them leaving the barn and Val going into the shower while Ryder cleaned up from the workout. He was eating his dinner. It was a sumptuous feast that his wife always seemed to make after she went out for an extra long session of errands. He had seconds.

His wife, normally not a woman of huge appetites, also had seconds and Mr. Kravitz thought she must have really worked up a powerful hunger doing all those hours of afternoon errands.

***

Ryder listened to the water from Val's shower going through the pipes. He knew the difference in sound from the hot water to the cold water. Contrary to what he told her to do, she only had a hot shower going.

Ryder opened the wood panel that hid the pipes in the wall and turned the red colored knob to the off position and within seconds heard Val scream in the shower. He knew she probably just put conditioner in her hair and would have to rinse it.

Ryder heard all the water turn off, the shower door open, and then an angry walk to the bathroom door, which Val opened, and then she yelled, "Where's the hot water? I have a head full of conditioner.!"

"Finish your shower, there's no more hot water."

"I can't finish my shower without -"

"Cold water is great for your muscles, your skin, your organs, your inner strength. I told you that."

"You!" Val yelled at him, finally realizing why there was no more hot water coming through the pipes.

"Yes, me." Ryder said with a smile.

"You!" Val was incensed but she also knew she could not win this battle.

"Do that breathing I taught you and it will help you deal with the cold. Use your inner strength. Let your mind keep you warm. Be the -"

Val loudly shut the bathroom door and was yelling obscenities in between mocking Ryder for 'trying to be a guru' and other statements. She wasn't happy with the situation but she tried.

As the cold water hit her skin they felt like a thousand needles, but she persisted in her breathing exercise and though the pain never stopped completely, it did lessen a little. She continued to persist and concentrate and breathe deliberately and deeply. And when it was over she felt a level of energy and a sense of alertness that she had not felt in quite a long time, if ever.

She emerged from the bathroom with a towel wrapped around her head and another one around her body. She went into the kitchen, and then the living room looking for Ryder. She called out, “Ryder!”

He was in his bedroom looking under his bed for an old box and was not in the mood for more of Val’s angry complaining about cold water during her shower, “Val, I’m in here, but I don’t want to hear anymore -”

“It worked!”

He crawled back out from under his bed, turned over and looked at her in her towel splendor. “It did?”

“Yes! It did!” Val said with a beaming smile that Ryder soon returned. “No one is more surprised about it than me!” Ryder laughed and then Val did too. She then looked him in the eyes seriously and said, “I want you to teach me more!”

***

Mrs. Kravitz kept a journal, not a diary, and after writing in it she would tear up the pages and throw them away. It was an unusual practice, but it made her feel better. After dinner she sat down in her special chair by the rear window that overlooked her backyard and got out her journal and special fountain pen. She then wrote a couple of paragraphs about how her favorite feature of Teddy was his ears. Not the way they looked, but the way they worked. Teddy listened to her. She was heard by him.

***

Val was outside walking throughout the garden, smelling flowers and trimming back bushes and branches. Ryder looked out of the window at her and felt something twist in his gut. It was that same, awful feeling overtaking him again. Ryder did not want to be this way, but at his age, he really liked his own routine and privacy. Ryder enjoyed his solitude, or maybe enjoy wasn't the most accurate word to describe what Ryder felt as he used to go about his days of solitude, but it was close.

Ryder felt a duty to Nick and his memory and so he bit his tongue and held back on his honest emotions the best he could, and did not ask Val pointedly when she was going back to her home. That was the question he pondered many times a day, but he would not let himself ask her.

But then he would think that maybe he should get a definite date on when she was going away. Was it a day or so? A week, maybe two weeks? It couldn't be a month, could it? Ryder was almost scared of the answer Val might give if he did ask that question. And he was nervous how he would react.

His Uncle William had passed away almost a decade ago so he couldn't call him and ask for counsel.

Even if his Mom was still alive she would not have known Nick well enough to answer best what to do and how to handle this house guest that just might be staying for a long, long time.

Ryder then thought about Leanne. It didn't take much for him to wander his psyche and soul back to her. As he began to meander down that memory lane he could hear her voice saying his name, and it was magical. He then could hear his own voice answering her back, in the much higher pitch of his sixteen year old self. He then saw her smiling at him and then had a visual picture of himself standing next to her, elated and proud. Knowing the world saw him better in her shadow.

Ryder began to do what he usually did in these moments, he opened his nightstand drawer and got out a folder of pictures from that early 1980s era. There they were, together, young, handsome and happy beyond belief. Unwrinkled. Unburdened. Unencumbered. Uncommon.

Ryder then began to talk out loud to her. That was one of the reasons he valued his privacy and did not like other eyes and ears in his house, he knew he was more than slightly crazy, just he had to be. Why else was he talking so naturally to someone he no longer really knew?

Ryder didn't know this, but Val had noticed, and heard him talking when he was alone. She heard him in his room chatting away and at first just figured he was talking on his cell phone, until she remembered he told her he had no cell phone. Val got up and checked the telephone that was attached to the wall in the kitchen and sure enough, there it was, still attached to the wall. So who was Ryder talking to, all alone? Val wondered about this but never could summon the courage to ask him. She felt it was a harmless aspect of his personality, though she did listen intently anytime he was in his bedroom to hear if it would happen again. It did. But Val could not make out enough words to really understand what Ryder was saying or who he was saying it to.

Now, Ryder shook away the nostalgia as it hurt too much despite the temporary respite of joy it gave him and got back into the present.

He knew who he should call. The only one left to call. The only one that would understand.

Ryder reached for the phone but then saw how late in the evening it was and knew he shouldn't bother to dial. Dave would be drunk. But not just slightly slurring drunk, he would be barely understandable and telling the same story three times drunk. Ryder made a mental note to call him tomorrow morning, early, before ten in the morning, before the first bottle was opened.

***

"There's nothing to eat here!" Val yelled as she rifled through Ryder's cupboards and refrigerator and pantry.

It was early morning and Ryder had just come back home from a hill repeat run. He thought he would be annoyed at Val complaining while being a guest in his house but he surprisingly wasn't. He had fought the urge to be vexed at her presence in his cabin many times. Today that mood of annoyance did not touch him."There's plenty to eat, you just don't want to eat it. Look," Ryder said, reaching into the pantry for a box of coconut BoBo protein bars, "these are delicious, I love them, try one!"

"I'm looking for food, not cardboard!"

"Unfair! They are so tasty."

"Let's go to your grocery store you work at and get some real food. Food with colors." Val pleaded.

"My protein bars are brown, that's a color." Ryder countered.

"How about some greens? Some veggies and fruits? Would I be overstepping my guest status to request some of those?"

Ryder shot a glance at the clock and thought about the call he wanted to make to Dave and how he only had so much sober time left to talk. "Ok, but let's hurry. I'll get you a bike from the Krammit Inn."

***

The Mountain Air Organic Grocer was located on the edge of town in a sprawling building that used to be a hotel/supply depot during the time of the great gold rush. Much of the ornate wood work remained intact as did the charm of its yesteryear heydays. Some of the shelves were original to the late 1800s and the layout of the store could be quite confusing for the new shoppers.

Some of the old hotel rooms were now being used for storage, but not all of the rooms. One still even had an original bed and bedroom set in it. That was suite 22.

Mesa and John/Sven were both working that morning at the grocer. Mesa was in the oils and herbs section while John/Sven worked both the register and helped unload a truck full of coffee shipments.

John/Sven looked at the clock and tried not to look across the store at Mesa, but it was getting increasingly difficult not to. He tried not to let himself even glance over at her. Not as his break time approached. He swore to himself he would have restraint and simply sit and read a book and maybe have some of that new coffee during his break.

Mesa also was very purposely not looking in the direction of the registers or the open door where the coffee truck was being unloaded, she knew very well what time it was. She also knew her appetite. She wanted masala tea, but also so much more. Mesa stopped running from who she was many decades ago.

With a flick of her long, wavy hair she turned and knew her colorful cashmere dress would also dance around her as she made her way to the old-fashioned sign in/sign out white board that the grocer had hung for its employees. Mesa wrote down the time she was starting her break and then deliberately strode over to the stairway and began to ascend the steps to the second floor.

John/Sven was powerless. He tried to find more duties to accomplish but it was no use and he resigned himself to his fate. It was a glorious fate and one that he revelled in, but still he sometimes wondered about the morality of it all. He was still running, occasionally, from who he was.

John/Sven wrote down his break time on the white board and then also ascended the same stairway that Mesa did. He then walked down the old fashioned and ornate hall, past the rooms that housed cans, boxes, bottles, and other sundries. John/Sven then made his way to room 22 where the door was slightly ajar and he entered it, locked it, and didn't emerge for half an hour.

***

When Ryder didn't see either of his friends working he peered at the white board and smiled knowingly. He then thought about it and laughed out loud causing Val to inquire why he did. "You're too young, you wouldn't understand." Ryder said laughing again and also ruffling her hair.

Val was not used to this silly side of Ryder but she liked it, even if her hair was now disheveled. He was a man of extreme moods, it seemed to her. He was hard to figure out, moment to moment. It was unnerving but also exciting, and a little bit exhausting too. But she was his guest, and she needed his expertise and guidance, so she rode whatever wave his ocean of emotion unleashed.

***

During the lull of activity in the neighborhood with Ryder and Val gone on their bikes to the store, Mr. Kravitz tried to assuage his conscience by offering to help his wife plant some flowers in the window boxes around the house. She accepted his assistance and for the rest of the morning both of them had clean consciousnesses.

***

Dave was just finishing his first Red Stripe beer so it was a perfect conversation in Ryder's opinion. How did Ryder know this? He could hear the second bottle top being opened and discarded on Dave's counter. Dave was loose enough from the first one to talk freely and give great advice. Had the call occurred a few hours later, well, Ryder was just happy it didn't.

"Help her anyway you feel comfortable doing. And not just for her sake, but I bet it'll make you feel better."

"You think?" Ryder asked as he stood in his kitchen and looked out the window at where Val was. Ryder wanted to make sure he wasn't being heard by her and with her straightening out some of the workout toys in the Kramit Inn he knew he wouldn't be. "So you think that I should -"

"You're always happier when you make someone else happy. Always." Dave said and he sounded more than a little melancholy.

Ryder knew not to ask what Dave would be doing for the rest of the day. The answer would be nothing. Nothing but drinking. Drinking and remembering. Maybe scrolling through old photos on his phone. He might go out to his favorite bar, or maybe a new one. Hopefully in an Uber.

Ryder knew Dave had lost his purpose, his drive to feel essential to someone, anyone. One day spilled into the next for Dave and it was heart wrenching to Ryder. And that's when Ryder got his answer.

It wasn't something he wanted to do, per se. And it sure wasn't a place he ever wanted to revisit. But taking Val, the daughter of his deceased friend Nick who was always so kind to him, back to the mountain that claimed him, well, that would be essential. And that would be a worthy purpose and a sacrifice for another.

Ryder knew in his heart but he didn't think it would be wise to share that decision with Val just yet.

***

Mrs. Kravitz rolled over onto her back, sweaty and panting lustily, and felt herself smiling as her eyes locked into the spinning blades of her weekend boyfriend's bedroom ceiling fan. Teddy seemed to always have the fan going, at least when she was over, and she wondered if Teddy knew that they would end up there, looking up with happy and spent expressions. She didn't mind one bit if Teddy was that presumptuous. Mrs. Kravitz enjoyed the feeling of being that valued.

As she lay there, catching her breath, she pictured Teddy getting his place ready for her arrival. She could see him pulling the lever for the ceiling fan to begin spinning, and then maybe cleaning and tidying up every room. Probably vacuuming and scrubbing the sinks and toilets as well.

She grinned up at the spinning faux bamboo blades and felt not the least bit guilty. She wondered if there was something wrong with her moral fiber that what she just did and who she did it with did not cause her even a pang of regret or a need for repentance. She thought of a possible sentence that a biographer might write about her and this particular moment, had she been noteworthy enough to warrant a biography. 'Despite the soiled sheets she had a clean conscience.'

Mrs. Kravitz now stopped grinning and furrowed her eyebrows, she did not like that sentence. Too graphic.

"What are you thinking about?" Teddy asked her and she was startled back to the reality of the moment. He had been watching her. He loved to watch her. He loved her. He wanted to tell her, and tell her often, but always chickened out.

Mrs. Kravitz turned to Teddy and studied his face. Her husband listened to this one song that talked about a 'handsome Dan' and she thought about it and that was not what Teddy was. She wasn't being mean in her assessment either. His figure for a man his age was passable. His face was average enough. It was his imploring eyes and his eager ears that not only attracted her initially but kept her coming back week after week. He deeply studied her features and listened to every word she uttered.

She now smiled again, and slowly leaned in to kiss him as much as a means to redirect the conversation as to show him affection.

"I like your ceiling fan." Mrs. Kravitz lied. She didn't like the ceiling fan, she thought the faux bamboo blades were trashy and cheap. What she did like was that he made sure they were on for her.

"You do?" Teddy asked brightly. "I got them because they reminded me of the ones in the movie 'Casablanca' with Bogart. We still have to see that one together, you know. Maybe some night -"

Mrs. Kravitz leaned in and kissed Teddy again, and again it was to redirect the conversation.

Staying that long and late as to watch a movie after all of their other activities just might make her feel guilty. She had enough negative and sad parts of her life, she didn't want any to creep into her Saturday afternoon visits with Teddy. It was why she never told Teddy she loved him, even though she thought she did, or at least might some day. She also was pretty sure Teddy loved her but she didn't want to hear him say it because that reality just might make her feel thoroughly guilty, and that would ruin everything. She could only do this if she maintained her clean conscience.

***

While sitting in his chair with his binoculars at the ready, Mr. Kravitz looked at his watch and noticed that his wife was still gone doing errands. The day had sort of gotten away from him and it was later in the afternoon than he thought it was. It was during this lull in his voyeuristic activities while no one was outside and so there was nothing to watch, that he finally missed his wife's company. He thought about how these past few months she had stopped nagging him and usually seemed to be cheery and bright. Mr. Kravitz thought about how nice it was to help his wife fill those flower boxes earlier that morning. There was a breezy repartee between them and he felt like they connected, just like in the old days of his more vigorous youth.

Mr. Kravitz did not know what could be filling his wife with so much effervescence but he was happy it was happening.

***

It was going to be an early morning start. Ryder softly knocked on Val's door and he told himself if she didn't respond and come out of the room ready to go then he would quietly leave without her. To his amazement, after the second knock on the door and before he could do a third, the bedroom door whirled open quickly which caused Ryder to jump back. "Good morning!" Val said a little too loudly for Ryder's liking, after just being scared and now embarrassed by it.

He fought against being defensive or in a bad mood and instead congratulated Val on her punctuality and jovialness at that early hour. "Yes it 'tis little Miss Sunshine! Aren't you full of vim and vigor!"

"Well it is almost five am, why wouldn't I be?" Val countered in full sarcastic mode, yet said with a smile.

They grabbed their water bottles and protein bars and headed out of Ryder's cabin but then stopped in his driveway before continuing into the forest. Both turned on their head lamps and put on their rucksacks full of weights. Ryder weighed in just over fifty pounds whereas Val's was just under forty. The goal was for four hours of ascending before a break. Ryder figured if Val could handle that…

They kept a slow but steady pace and the few instances of talk that occurred between them was usually Ryder encouraging Val and inquiring about how she was holding up and her saying she was doing just fine.

As they cleared yet another steep ridge Val kept her strides constant but Ryder stopped and let his rucksack slip to the ground. Val heard the sound of his rucksack hitting the rock below him and now looked up and turned around.

Ryder was smiling at her.

"We're here." Ryder said triumphantly and then laid down and rested his head on his rucksack like a pillow. Through closed eyes he heard her do the same. "Isn't it gorgeous up here?" Ryder asked, never opening his eyes.

Having been fooled repeatedly by false summits, she was surprised they were actually really at the top. Val lifted herself up on her elbows, took in the expansive vista of endless mountains and trees, and simply said, "Yes." Val plopped back down and used this time to catch her breath and rest her leg muscles.

After a few moments Ryder spoke with his eyes still closed and his body unmoved from before, "Should we eat?"

"Wait until I regain consciousness." Val joked more out of habit than reality, she actually felt pretty good, all things considered. The amount of work she had been putting in at the Krammit Inn as well as the forest, coupled with her newly discovered clean diet, had really begun to pay dividends.

Ryder now sat up and looked around at their surroundings on the summit. "This never gets boring."

Val looked around too and agreed. "Nope." Val then reached into her rucksack and got out a BoBo coconut oatmeal bar and unwrapped it and then popped a quarter of it into her hungry mouth.

Ryder's lips moved but Val could not hear him saying anything. She kept watching him do this and then he smiled, more to himself than to her. He then said something else basically just to himself, and then he noticed Val looking at him. Ryder got very self-conscious and pointed to the sky in order to change the subject, "Looks clear." he replied, stating the obvious and not hiding what she saw.

Val's mind went back to all the times she heard Ryder talking to either himself or maybe to an imaginary friend, or a ghost from the past. She didn't know which one it was. She also didn't know if she wanted to ask him about it.

"Yes, pretty clear." Val said and let him off the hook. She would not intrude on his psychosis this morning.

"Ahhhh." Ryder moaned in delight.

"You really should have a dog. A dog would love this! A dog would love this hike and be great company for you." Val said, thinking she was helping.

"I told you, I had one." Ryder sighed.

"I know, but I'm not going to be forever and -"

"You promise?" Ryder joked, or at least Val hoped he was joking.

"This way you wouldn't be alone. And like I said, I know a dog would love this life you're living here!"

"I'm kind of a one and done kind of guy. I loved that dog I had, I don't think I can love another. It'd be too hard, hurt too much. I don't know."

Ryder laid and thought and Val did not pursue it anymore. Sometimes, she was learning, silence is better.

The rest time on the summit was brief and soon they were barrelling down the same trail they had ascended earlier. The slightly less than four hours upwards was only about an hour on the descent.

Ryder stopped Val by the banks of a stream that was full of ice cold water that was rushing by from the spring melt off. "Now for the really fun part!" Ryder said and dropped his rucksack.

Val had no idea exactly what he meant and wondered if he was going to make a pass at her. If he did, she wasn't sure if she would have minded.

"Fun part?" Val asked as she watched him now take off his shirt, and then his socks, and then his shorts.

"What are you waiting for?" Ryder asked, seeing Val standing still on the edge of the stream in a grassy patch.

"What the -"

"For your body. It's what you need." Ryder explained but Val still looked confused.

"What I need?" Val asked as Ryder was now wearing only his short, tight fitting, black silk boxers that showed off his muscular legs. Now she revisited the question she posed to herself before, and thought that if he did hit on her she would put up not an ounce of resistance and see where it all led.

Val had been alone for the past year after breaking up with yet another dead end boyfriend. Ryder was a lot of things, but he was no dead end. He might have been older than her by twelve or so years, but he was in excellent shape. He obviously invested well and had money too. She was intrigued. She was suddenly excited. She hadn't had an outdoor adventure like this in way too many years! She noticed her throat was dry and her forehead was perspiring more than when she was hiking.

"It'll take just ten minutes!" Ryder exclaimed and got a towel out of his rucksack and laid it on the patch of grass. Val thought that last sentence was not really a selling point to what she thought he had in mind.

"My Uncle William showed me this, and your Dad and Dave too!" Val's mood was now turned in a different direction. Ryder walked into the stream and quickly sat down in it and yelled from the frigid waves splashing all over him. "Come on in! You can leave a couple of things on but get in!"

Val felt foolish in her vanity. Of course, it was not a come on session at all, but a wellness experience. She took off her shirt but left on her sports bra. She took off her shoes and then socks but left on her shorts. She hesitated, fearing the cold water onslaught, but then plowed in and sat down right next to Ryder and screamed much louder than he did. And they both laughed.

The almost freezing rush of water on her scantily clad body did feel refreshing and exhilarating. Val never knew mornings in such uncomfortable circumstances and positions could be so gratifying and satisfying. It had been another arduous week of rope climbing, tire flipping and other strength training exercises all the while hiking, hiking, and more hiking. "Inclines are your friend!" Ryder said so often Val thought it just might be his mantra. Her aching body responded to the healing waters of the beautiful forest stream and she suddenly felt she could accomplish anything.

While in the stream her thoughts were kept right there in the liquid arctic blast that was hitting her overworked body. But after she had dried herself off, with a towel that Ryder had considerately packed for her in his rucksack, and put her shirt back on she began to revisit the previous topic that was running through her brain - should she accept a sexual invitation from Ryder.

She prided herself on a very healthy appetite for those sorts of physical adventures since she was a high school upperclassmen though she had to admit that more often than not it got her into trouble, and some awful relationships. Would being that way with Ryder wreck her plans to go to Tibet? What if they got together but then broke up right before they departed for Asia, that sure could make a trip uncomfortable, or even cancelled!

They began to walk back to Ryder's cabin, still shivering and goose pimpled but rejuvenated.

Val slowed herself down with the realization that he hadn't even made an offer for such things. Wait, she pondered, why was that? Could he not be interested in her? Her, a younger and shapely, nicely put together woman. That thought brought her down a peg or two. Or maybe he's gay and just not interested in anyone from her team. Or maybe he's in love with another woman.

Val thought that would explain it. It would explain a lot. But who would this mystery woman be?

Then it was obvious to her, of course, Mesa!

Val thought that Mesa oozed sexuality and laughed a little too freely at Ryder's jokes and seemed to make any time the right time to subtly touch his arm or shoulder. One time she even rubbed his chest and commented on how strong he was and that he should invest in cashmere sweaters because they were the sexiest on a hard body like his! Val thought Mesa was not exactly subtle! Val could see it a mile away now, it was all so clear! Ryder couldn't make a move on her because he was involved with Mesa.

As they approached the cabin they both stopped to take off some of their wet outer garments and shoes and hung them on the line to dry. Mr. Kravitz scooted up in his chair and put down his cup of coffee and then lifted up his binoculars.

Val looked carefully at Ryder when she asked him, "So, any plans on seeing Mesa tonight?" Val wanted to see if he would betray his lust for her through his eyes or through his voice.

Val did not detect anything of a steamy nature to his reply when he answered, "None that I know of."

***

Mesa loved the warm morning breeze that entered her open windows and caressed her exposed skin. It was her favorite way to wake up.

She softly took a breath in through her nose and then held it for a few beats and then let it out of her mouth. She then took a deeper breath and held it longer before letting it out in a long exhale.

Mesa then put her hands on her heart. She closed her eyes and then let her fingers travel all over her body as her breathing continued in a powerful and fulfilling way. Mesa then whispered out loud for only herself and the universe to hear, "Today I am grateful for …" and then listed three things, one that had yet to happen, that she was grateful for. This was called future pacing.

Mesa took her time and savored the moment alone with herself. She then whispered three things that she celebrated about herself and was proud of. Her mind stayed focused and clear.

She then brought her knees to her chest and held them there for a few wonderful beats before letting them go. "Today, I desire …" Mesa again whispered and then said quietly the three things she really wanted, including one that she felt might sound out of reach but that she desired just the same.

Mesa now stretched slowly, this way and that way, and closed her eyes and enjoyed her own touch.

Lastly Mesa now softly said to herself, "I deeply and profoundly accept, respect, forgive, and love you!"

She rolled out of bed with a soulful smile and felt armed and equipped with what she needed to start her day with.

***

Had Val asked, Ryder would have been happy to tell her some of what she wanted to know. Some.

No, he was not gay and never had ever been attracted to men. No, he was not involved with Mesa. He did also think, as did Val, that Mesa oozed sexuality and would be an amazing partner for many athletic and amorous adventures but not for him. Occasionally his mind went there, though, when he'd see her doing her yoga in her colorful garb and her sultry movements would let him lose himself in her erotic ways and enticing presence. He would temporarily forget the walls that the past put up. But those moments were fleeting.

When Val said she was going to lay in the hammock that was strung between two shady trees in the backyard and read a novel set in Tibet during the 1950s, Ryder knew that he'd have some alone time.

He briefly let his mind wonder about what Val might be like in that context, that of being more than just a friend. He was no fan of vaping nor tattoos and there was something else he just couldn't put his finger on that kept him from being interested in her in that way. He didn't want to complicate things either.

Ryder did have to admit that Val did look amazingly fit when they did their polar plunge in the icy river. He noticed that through their various workouts she had retained her alluring curves but also tightened the parts of the body that looked more appealing when tightened. She really was a gorgeous and comely younger woman.

But Ryder shook his head to rid his mind of such thoughts. He didn't know exactly why he felt wrong thinking about them, but he just did.

He reached into his night stand and pulled out a folder of four decades old letters and pictures. He closed his door and then kicked off his shoes. Ryder propped up his pillow and reclined on his bed and began to pursue the contents that he wanted to keep secret and known only to himself.

***

John/Sven looked at his phone and saw that it was time for another set. His training buddy stood up and readied himself to spot John/Sven on his last set of bench presses, though the friend knew if anything went wrong he could never lift that bar of weights alone. John/Sven was benching almost three hundred pounds!

In the five years since he moved out to Crested Butte to live with his Dad, John/Sven had put on seventy pounds of muscle and had many dalliances with older women. He thought the former probably led to the latter. His light blonde hair, dimples, and massive frame was like catnip to the over thirty-five years old crowd of women he encountered. John/Sven learned of love and loved and learned. It was the one education he actually enjoyed. His college semester was a failure.

John/Sven was blessed with just enough money that he didn't have to work full-time but not enough that he didn't have to work at least part-time. Ryder thought his friend had it too comfortable, "Svenny, you know, comfort is cancer! You need a mortgage, that'd light a fire under you!"

John/Sven would laugh, nod, and acknowledge to Ryder, "Yes, you are probably right." Yet not change anything.

John/Sven was coasting through life. It wasn't a bad thing, necessarily, but it did gnaw at him sometimes.

He thought he might want to be a real estate agent, took the test three times and finally passed. Four months and only one house sale later he was studying for the LSAT to see if he could get into Law School and become a lawyer. After his test score left him in the bottom ten percent, and having not graduated from college, he then turned his direction to finance.

He was comfortable, and having much more fun than most, so why would he upset the apple cart and change?

John/Sven finished his last set, took a shower, and then set off to the grocery store where he worked part time, under the guise of looking at the work schedule to see when his next shift would be. If he also saw a certain comely, older yoga practicing woman in long flowing and colorful garb, well then…

***

FLORIDA GULFCOAST
APRIL, 1982

"Don't worry, Mom, I'll be back way before noon!"

"You better be, your plane takes off -"

"Let the boy be. My nephew can be trusted to be on time." Uncle William said to his sister as Ryder stood anxiously and impatiently by the front door with his backpack on. Uncle William waved him on but the teenager would not leave his house until his mother gave her blessing.

With a smile and a nod she did and he hugged her one more time, then he shook his uncle's hand, and was gone in a flash. It was early evening and Ryder had just finished having a farewell dinner with his mother and Uncle William the night before the Tibet trip. He was packed and ready so why shouldn't he sleep over at his buddy's house and see his friends one last night.

Ryder had the plan all worked out in his head and with his best friend Billy as well. It was a perfect subterfuge. Ryder thought nothing could go wrong and that he had worked out every detail.

Ryder felt like Billy's house was a second home and that familiarity led him to not even knock when he arrived there. Ryder just walked in and jauntily said in a faux Australian accent, "Ello Misses Smith!"

Billy's mom put down her dish towel and waved to Ryder and motioned for him to come into the kitchen where she was cleaning up after dinner.

"Are you really going through with this?" Mrs. Smith asked as Ryder opened the refrigerator even though he wasn't the least bit hungry, it was just a habit. Seeing him do this she playfully yelled at him, "Get out of there!"

"Yes, of course, mountains are my business!" Ryder answered back and then added, "So is danger!"

Billy came into the kitchen with several fishing poles and a tackle box and after he kissed his mother goodbye they were quickly in Billy's 1973 Gran Torino and speeding down the street in that blue and silver muscle car.

They went over all the details of the coming night and then after Billy made a couple of more right hand turns they were at the Sunset Pier. Billy parked right next to Steve's car, an inauspicious red 1978 Dodge Omni.

Steve's car was empty as he was already set up on the pier with all of his fishing gear. Billy and Ryder took their gear and walked up to their friend and Ryder yelled out to him, "Zander!"

Ryder liked to call Steve 'Zander' because he thought his friend looked a lot like Robin Zander, the heartthrob lead singer for the rock group Cheap Trick. Billy agreed. But neither Billy nor Ryder liked this fact seeing as all the girls seemed to gravitate to the photogenic and over six feet tall Steve.

"You are a crazy swiney pig!" Steve said back to Ryder as they shook hands in the current way teenagers did.

"What you talking 'bout Willis?" Ryder asked back with a smile and then puffed up his cheeks to try to look like Gary Coleman who was a popular television child actor of that era.

"Crazy swiney pig!" Steve just repeated.

"My trip to Tibet?" Ryder wondered but then Steve shook his head 'no'. "You are a crazy swiney pig!"

The boys set up their fishing poles and got out some of the lemonade Billy's mother made for them and talked, and cast, and joked, and cast, and occasionally one of them got a bit on the line. Darkness came and Billy now began to pour a lot of the chum they got from the local grocery store, Winn Dixie, off the side of the pier and into the sea. They also changed the fishing poles they were using along with the bait, they were now shark fishing.

This went on for a while until Ryder asked Billy what time it was and Billy smiled and slyly answered, "It's time. Oh, it's time."

Ryder smiled and then gave Steve a quick hug. "Have fun, Ryder. Have fun in Tibet too, you swiney pig!"

"Crazy swiney pig!" Ryder corrected him and then left with Billy in the darkness and left the pier and went back to Billy's car.

They drove a couple of miles until Billy cut the engine, turned off his lights, and coasted past a few houses.

"Billy Boy, I really appreciate this." Ryder said quietly and sincerely. He then got his backpack out of the backseat. Ryder checked his hair in the side passenger mirror and got his comb out of the back pocket of his blue jeans and made everything look to his satisfaction. "Gotta check the ole' hair situation!"

"Gotta!" Billy said and laughed. "I'd say 'have fun' but I'm guessing there's no need to say that!"

"Thanks pal! See you tomorrow morning! Don't forget to leave your window unlocked. Or I'm -"

"Dude, it's already unlocked."

"You rule!" Ryder said and with that he disappeared around a hedge and Billy could no longer see him so he drove back to the pier to continue shark fishing with Steve.

Ryder tiptoed through the side driveway and stealthily made his way under the elevated back porch, where the long ladder was kept on hooks at the Rhobbs household. The large and imposing two story, five bedroom house was well-known to Ryder these past few months. He knew the layout and also the sleep schedules and nocturnal activities of Mr. and Mrs. Rhobbs. When the father, a lawyer, was there and not on a business trip, he went to sleep first followed shortly after by the mother. The mother, a civil service worker for the county, though, always seemed to wake up around 2pm and roamed the house briefly.

Normally on a typical night when Ryder was still in the Rhobbs living room with Leanne this is when she would quietly yet sternly admonish him for still being there and to get home now!

The time now was just past midnight and Ryder knew this was a quiet period of the night and so he gingerly lifted the long ladder off of its hooks and carried it back around the corner and to the driveway. Ryder then walked a little further and gently placed the ladder on the wall just under a window, which instantly opened! Leanne's smiling face was then seen by Ryder to be beaming at him from above. "You made it, sugar!" Leanne exclaimed in a whisper that Ryder still thought was too loud.

"Shhh, my love!" Ryder tried to reprimand her in his sweetest voice. To be caught, Ryder felt, would be left to a fate worse than death.

He climbed the ladder and she was kissing him before he even started to make his way through the window and into her bedroom. He felt bad he couldn't kiss her back, yet, but he had to concentrate on both getting safely through the bedroom window and also accomplishing that task quietly.

The moment he fell on her bedroom floor she quickly and quietly closed the window and was on top of him kissing him, and this time, safely ensconced in her bedroom, he could return her fervor.

But then he noticed the taste of salt and he backed his face up just a bit to look at her. "You're crying?"

"I'm going to miss you so much!" Leanne exclaimed and then began to sob heavily while hugging Ryder as tight as she could.

Ryder tried to kiss her tears away but that only seemed to make more appear. "I'll come back to you." Ryder quietly pledged.

"Promise?" Leanne asked while wiping her nose on her sleeve and not caring a whit about not being ladylike.

"I swear to God." Ryder declared. "Nothing will ever keep me from you. Nothing." Ryder said and kissed her. "Ever." Another kiss. "Will ever keep me." A longer kiss. "From you." They were intertwined for a deliciously glorious time and then Leanne led Ryder off of her bedroom floor and onto a more comfortable place for recumbent.

***

CRESTED BUTTE, COLORADO
APRIL, 2019

Val, Ryder, and two of his other friends Seth and Nicole, were all lying on the floor of the Krammit Inn in a half-circle with their faces down on the ground and their buttocks sticking up into the air. Mesa was at the head of the room and demonstrating this position and she guided the breathing she wanted them to focus on. John/Sven bowed out of this activity and instead was lifting an obscene amount of weight over his head with just one of his large arms. It was night time and the lights in the Krammit Inn were on but they were dimmed to a low setting to provide ambiance.

There was just enough illumination for Mr. Kravitz, nestled in his chair across the seat to monitor all the movements through his binoculars. He was too busy to notice the late hour that his wife was still out doing errands in.

Val enjoyed this yoga session much more than Ryder did, and she now began to enjoy Mesa's company much more than she did when she first met her and considered her a rival for Ryder's attention and possibly affection. Val was impressed by the depth of spirituality that Mesa possessed and tried to pass on to others through her yoga sessions.

Earlier, they had all taken turns trying to climb the rope that Ryder had attached to the top of his barn. Mesa could not get off the ground unless she jumped. John/Sven made it three arms lengths before his great bulk caused him to return to Earth. The same thing happened to Ryder's guiding friend Seth. Seth's wife Nicole and Ryder both easily made it to the top of the ceiling and each came down carefully and effectively. Val then started her ascent and just about made it before she began to waiver in her belief, and her strength, and then retreated back down the rope.

It was a good test of their upper body strength in relation to their weight. The yoga after this was welcome

The different poses and exercises were surprisingly strenuous but Val was adept and more elastic than she thought she would be. Ryder muddled through the set and looked forward to the cool down, that was his favorite part!

The cool down this night consisted of the participants resting their legs over the seat of a chair while their backs were on the ground and their arms were stretched out wide on the floor. Mesa whispered that they should close their eyes and take deep and lasting breaths. She then continued to whisper to them and gave them congratulations for what they accomplished and also affirmations for what was to be. Mesa then quietly moved to each person - John/Sven now joined the others laying on the floor - and softly put her hands first onto their foreheads and then tenderly held her hand to their hearts. It was a soul sharing experience that moved them all, but Val most of all.

Val felt tears dropping down her cheeks from her closed eyes as she let go of previous pains and traumas and looked expectantly to future joys and triumphs. Mesa noticed this and doubled back to Val and reached down and held both of Val's hands in hers, and then kissed them.

Mesa then gently guided Val's hands back to the floor and resumed her place at the head of the semi-circle. In her melodious murmur, Mesa then began to chant a positive incantation.

This went on long enough for everyone there to have a relaxing and rejuvenating cool down. Mesa then sat up straight with her legs intertwined underneath herself and smiled at everyone. "Come in." Mesa quietly asked and motioned with her hands and the six of them all met in the middle of the circle for a group hug.

Mr. Kravitz was so enraptured in what he was viewing from across the street that he never heard his wife finally come home from her full, vigorous day of 'errands' and enter the living room.

"Haven't you moved-" Mrs. Kravitz began to say to her husband who was so startled he jumped so violently his binoculars banged against the picture window though thankfully did not shatter it.

***

FLORIDA GULFCOAST
JULY, 1982

Leanne was conflicted. Usually when she was in over her head and full of anxiety over something all she had to do was picture Ryder and her together and she would calm down and smile and be fine. Now, when she recalled their last night together, rather than soothe her nerves it caused her even more consternation.

She thought back first on that night before he left for Tibet when Ryder snuck into her room through her window and the four magical times that they… Leanne couldn't help but smile and sigh.

But then she recalled what happened the next morning after her alarm clock went off at five am. She cried, and held him tightly, and then he cried. They held each other but then heard some movement in the house and knew he had to make his getaway before her parents started their pre-work morning routine and discovered him there.

As Ryder descended the ladder that was still perched against her house and just under Leanne's bedroom window, a police car sped to a halt just at the entrance of the driveway. Ryder heard it and looked back, terrified, and then looked at Leanne who also saw it and was in shock.

Ryder forced a smile to Leanne and whispered, "It'll be alright, I promise." Ryder then hopped off the final rung of the ladder and calmly walked over to the officer who sternly approached with a drawn gun.

"Stop!" The officer commanded and Ryder obeyed. Ryder also put his hands up before the police man could ask.

"I'm not a robber." Ryder explained, forcing himself to stay calm and not sound guilty or flustered.

"What are you doing coming down a ladder at five am then?"

"I can explain, sir."

"We got a call from a neighbor, said she saw a ladder against the house and it looked suspicious."

"That's my girlfriend, Leanne Rhobbs, " Ryder said and turned and pointed to his girlfriend who was kneeling in her bedroom window, petrified and with tears still streaming down her face. "Wave to the officer Leanne."

Leanne waved with one hand and wiped away tears with the other.

"I'm leaving for Tibet later today with my uncle," Ryder continued to explain to the young officer, "and I snuck over to say goodbye to my girlfriend one last time. I'm not going to see you for a couple of months. We're in love, sir. And her parents hate me. And-"

The officer knew instantly that Ryder was not a robber but he had to be official. "Do you have any identification on you?"

"I have my driver's license." Ryder said and then pulled it out of his wallet to show the officer.

"Wait here." The police man said and then went back to his squad car to run the information Ryder gave him through the dispatch team back at the station. As he did this Leanne was panic-stricken that her parents were going to walk outside at any second and see what was occurring and that Ryder had spent the night with her.

The 24 year old police man was young enough that he remembered those romantic days of youth when one was in love despite the opposition of parents. Had this policeman been a bit older, a little bitter or jaded, maybe going through a divorce, this encounter could have instead turned dark quickly.

Once Ryder's information proved he was a law abiding teenager the officer returned his driver's license to him and put his hand on Ryder's shoulder and advised, "Say one more goodbye to your girlfriend then quietly be on your way home."

"Oh my goodness, thank you officer!"

"Do you have a way home?"

"My feet!"

"I'll drop you off. Good ahead." The officer said, nodding towards Leanne in her bedroom window.

Ryder ran over to the ladder, climbed it stealthily, kissed her one more time and smiled and said, "I told you it'd be fine!"

"I love you, sugar!"

"I love you, m'sweet!" Ryder said and then quickly climbed down and started towards the officer when he remembered he had to put away the ladder.

"I'll help you with that." The kindly policeman offered and together they quietly hung the ladder up.

Two months later, with Ryder in Tibet, Leanne was still worried that whichever neighbor called the police about the ladder just might mention the incident to her parents. So far that hasn't happened.

But as the weeks went by with Ryder gone, and no letters from him arriving from that far off country, she became more and more worried. So worried she often felt nauseous, weak, and very sleepy and tired.

Leanne did her best to try and stay busy but often she just napped and rested. Her parents noticed and figured she was just a love sick puppy who was depressed that her boyfriend was far away. They weren't depressed about Ryder being far away, they loved that fact!

Leanne then noticed something about her body. And noticed that something was missing and hadn't arrived like it should. She chalked this up to worry and depression as well. When even more weeks went by without getting it, or any letters from Ryder, she began to have more than just trepidation about what may be happening to her body. After sneaking out to a drug store her nervousness turned to horror when the green stripe proved that her fears were not unfounded.

She sat in her bedroom near the window where Ryder had snuck into, and cried for the rest of the afternoon.

Leanne had never been close to her older sister Jolene. Jolene was a narcissist, self-centered, dishonest, and much too pretty and curvy for her own good. But when Jolene got home from an excursion to the beach with a group of friends Leanne sought her out.

Leanne had remembered that Jolene had a friend that had a sister that had gotten 'into trouble' and somehow, someway figured out a way not to be 'in trouble' anymore.

Jolene was changing out of her swim suit when Leanne barged in without even knocking.

"What the h-" Jolene began to yell but then she saw the look of despair and the tears on her younger sister's face. Something familial stirred in her and she didn't continue yelling at Leanne. Instead, she took Leanne into her arms and hugged and with real concern asked her, "What's wrong?"

After Leanne explained it all to her sister, Jolene called her friend and got all the details she needed.

Everything was set for the next day.

As Leanne lay in bed, crying and praying, she wondered just why this all happened to her and where Ryder was and why hadn't she heard from him? Leanne had been writing him letters every day and putting them in a separate envelope marked with the appropriate date so when he came back to her from Tibet he could read them all in order. He promised to write to her faithfully and mail them from wherever he was so she could have some words from him and know he was alright.

Where were his letters? It had been two months.

She felt horribly alone.

She also felt horrible about herself and what she was about to do about the situation of her being 'in trouble'. Is that what Ryder would want her to do? She had no way of asking him or knowing.

Leanne literally cried herself to sleep that night and when Jolene woke her sister up the next morning she was shocked at how puffy Leanne's eyes were, and how empty and lifeless they looked.

They left together for their appointment.

Leanne was back home and crying, and then eventually sleeping, in her bed just after noon.

For the next three days she walked around, when she was on her feet, like she was in a fog.

Looking at Ryder's picture made everything better, and then worse.

Re-reading all of his love letters to her from the past made everything better, and then worse.

Listening to the cassette tapes of songs they both loved that he made for her made everything better, and then worse.

Leanne needed some current contact with him, or at least someone close to him, and so she dialed Ryder's home phone number.

"Hello?"

"Mrs. Nowacki? It's Leanne Rhobbs. I'm sorry I -"

"Oh my, Leanne, I meant to call you!" Mrs. Nowacki said frantically.

"What is it?" Leanne asked, suddenly fearing the worst.

"Ryder has been hurt in an avalanche. I got a call from the consulate yesterday evening. He's alright, they think, but the reports are sketchy. I have more calls in to our ambassador in Tibet."

"Oh my God, no!" Leanne screamed as her emotions again overtook her.

"Leanne! So far I've heard he's fine, just scrapes and bruises. He's fine, Leanne, he's ok." Mrs. Nowacki tried to effectively explain and soothe her son's girlfriend who sounded inconsolable. "One of the men they were with died, it's tragic and so sad! But not Ryder, he's alive and well."

Not much was registering inside Leanne's mind, except that Ryder was hurt and it was all her fault for what she had done to their baby.

Their baby.

What would have been their baby. And now would never be their baby because of what she did, without even talking to him.

CRESTED BUTTE, COLORADO
JUNE, 2019

Ryder was startled at how ecstatic and emotional Val got on that mountain summit when he finally told her that they were going to Tibet together in late October. It was the first time he had formally declared that fact to her and she jumped and shouted with joy. . He just figured by then it was a foregone conclusion that he would guide her.

They had both just taken an early morning hike up a moderate mountain to experience the colorful explosion of the wildflowers in near peak bloom. What Fall is to the Adirondack mountains and the kaleidoscope of colors that explode everywhere, late June and early July in Crested Butte is comparable.

Ryder knew with the late snow melt that the best places to view the wildflowers would be in Gunnison Valley and especially at Hartmann Rocks and Signal Peak. He had personally packed both of their backpacks with food and some extra clothing, you just never know what kind of weather might develop, and they had started out while everything was still dark. By the time they entered the valley Val was thunderstruck at the propensity of purple from the Silvery Lupines.

Val was transfixed at the sheer volume of this flower and the three shades it exhibited, silvery purple, magenta, and dark purple. Val loved how the flowers were tall with showy spikes of blooms. When Val examined the flowers closer she noticed the blooms themselves were dense with elongated clusters of pea-shaped flowers. She was about to snap off some for a bouquet but Ryder quickly told her that that is now allowed. Too many people picking the wildflowers could ruin the ecosystem and damage the fragile environment. Plus, you could get a ticket if you are caught picking them.

The rich, purple Larkspur and the red Indian Paintbrush were also in abundance but it took Ryder quite a bit of shady sleuthing to find the pink Calypso Orchid down near Cement Creek.

"I think these are my favorites!" Val exclaimed when Ryder pointed out a clump of two near the creek and under a tree. "I love the name too, the Calypso Orchid, sounds like a tropical drink!"

Ryder laughed and then added, "They're also called fairy slippers." Ryder enjoyed being her guide on this vegetation excursion.

"Fairy slippers? Now I like them even more!"

"I thought you might."

Val now stopped, put her hands on her hips, looked around and said to Ryder, "If only you got another dog…she would love it here!"

Ryder looked down and sort of smiled ruefully and yet playfully. He honestly replied, "If I wasn't such a one and done kind of guy."

Val left it alone.

They continued their hike amidst the grandeur of mother nature in that magical summer month.

It was at the peak of one of the gentle but picturesque hills that Ryder had spread out their lunch and then informed Val casually that he would guide her to Tibet. First his words did not register.

"This place looks like Tibet?" Val asked, hearing him completely wrong because honestly she was paying more attention to the sandwich she was unwrapping than the words he was saying.

When he repeated himself and she finally heard him accurately and now understood the enormity of his words she leaped up high and screamed a jubilatory "Waa-hoo!" Ryder couldn't help but think back on her father and when he talked about the Cleveland Indians mascot Chief Waa-Hoo.

Val then hugged Ryder and said "Thank you!" Over and over and over again. Then she was silent and still.

Ryder looked at her and was not sure what exactly she was thinking, be it good or bad, he couldn't tell.

Val sat back down, with her head down, but didn't eat her sandwich. She just sat in quiet contemplation.

Ryder thought he now understood. "Are you having second thoughts?" Ryder stood and waited a few moments for her to reply. She was in deep thought. "Are you scared? Do you think that maybe-"

"I am a little scared, like, what if I can't climb like I think I can or the thin air wrecks my lungs, or -"

"Don't turn yourself into knots now, here, before we get there. There's only one way to find out. You've put the work in. I believe in you."

Those last words hit Val hard, because she knew he did. She had earned his belief, and trust.

Her emotions came out honestly and with copious amounts of tears. Ryder was never comfortable with tears.

He had to make a joke, "Don't cry Val,you're going to cause a mud slide with all those tears."

It was a few minutes and bites of her sandwich later that she got down to the heart of the matter, "What if I can't handle seeing my dad's…" Val's voice trailed off. She shook her head and couldn't say the words.

"Burial place?" Ryder tenderly asked.

"If I can't even say it now, here, how will I be able to see it and experience it when we're there on the mountain? In freaking Tibet!"

Ryder sat down next to her and searched his mind, and then heart and soul, for the right words. "I don't know. I don't. I don't know how I'm going to be or react seeing that place again." Ryder lifted up her chin with his hand, softly, and they locked eyes, "But just know, we'll be there together."

Val's tears started again and she hugged him.

Ryder hugged her back and then, because he got uneasy around naked emotion, laughed and said, "No! I don't want another mud slide!"

SOMEWHERE OVER THE ATLANTIC OCEAN
JULY, 1982

Flying back to America, Ryder thought the carnage on the mountain was awful, and it was, but then there was another type of awful, and that was the days upon days he had to spend in the hospital. Not just any hospital, but a third world hospital where he did not speak the language and sterile surroundings were just a pipe dream. He lay in his hospital bed and replayed the avalanche and the aftermath. He had nothing else to do. There was nobody there that spoke English. He did not know where his Uncle William or Dave were in the hospital and nobody knew enough English to tell him.

A week later an official from the United States Consulate paid him a visit and gave him back his passports and also his new travel plans. He had a flight out of Kathmandu the next day that would take him to Doha, and then to New York and then back to Florida and his beloved Leanne.

Now on the airplane, unable to sleep as he was sandwiched between two smelly snoring bearded men, he thought back on all the devastation he witnessed both on the mountain as well as in that third world hospital.

Ryder was never one for hospitals, or doctors, or people moaning in agony or writhing in pain, but he got a steady dose of it in that hospital and all without air conditioning or proper ventilation.

He still didn't know what was happening with his Uncle William or Dave and that uncertainty of their conditions gnawed at him. At least the state official from the consulate told him that he would contact his mother so that put him at ease knowing she would know he was alright. He hoped maybe his mother would also call Leanne and let her know he was alright as well.

Leanne.

Just thinking about her made everything seem worthwhile and every problem concurable.

Leanne. He could just about picture her laying out next to her swimming pool in that cute little black bathing suit of hers. Just enjoying her carefree summer vacation while he first roasted in a dirty hospital and then spent most of a day and night flying over an ocean while being squished between…

He couldn't wait to see Leanne, he needed to see her smile and feel her happily hug his sorrows away.

***

CRESTED BUTTE, COLORADO
JULY, 1982

After Ryder dropped Val off at the airport in John/Sven's car that he borrowed and then returned to his now empty home, he could not shake this unsettled feeling. He finally had his cabin back, all to himself, and yet he wandered from room to room without any real purpose. Ryder felt off, a feeling he couldn't remember having in his cabin alone before.

Val had returned to Cleveland for two weeks to spend some time with her mother Susan and to also gather up all of the clothes she would need for her Tibetan quest. While she was eager to see her mother she had a feeling that there was a rope tied to her waist and it was pulling her back to the majestic mountains and rustic charm of Crested Butte, or was it back to Ryder?

Ryder for his part found himself on that first free morning, after his workout in the Krammit Inn, pursuing the websites that offered to pair families and homes for needy dogs. He then went into his room and opened his night stand and got out his folder of past pictures. After a few minutes he placed the pictures back into his night stand and wandered around aimlessly some more, looking for a purpose. Or was he looking for Val? Did he miss her? Did he miss sharing his freedom?

Ryder knew easy answers were not going to come from walking from room to room, he instead got his bicycle down from its resting place on a hook high on a side wall. Ryder then grabbed a BoBo bar and zipped it into his shorts pocket. An icy bottle of water was made next and attached to his bicycle, just below the handle bars.

Ryder stopped on the way out and looked at himself in the mirror and recognized the face and form but not the person.

***

The clock ticked slow for both Ryder and Val those two weeks.

Unbeknownst to Val, Ryder had shaved his head to a closely cropped style. He thought that might jar him out of his lethargy and confusion. It was a wasted effort that would take weeks to grow out.

Unbeknownst to Ryder, Val ditched her Joan Jett style spikey haircut for a much softer and gentle coif. Val did not want to admit to herself how much she liked the change. Her mother congratulated her on a great hair style choice. This new style would be easier to travel with though she feared Ryder would laugh and make fun of her. Maybe he would mock her for trying to 'look like a girl'.

Val also went out shopping with a friend to buy some better travel clothes that were of a lighter and quick drying material. Her friend suggested some more flowy and feminine styles that the Val who first came to Crested Butte might not have chosen, but the current amelioration of Valerie Brown did.

When he picked her up, finally, from the airport he was silent at first upon seeing her new look. Val was hoping he would say an instant compliment about the change she orchestrated, mostly on his behalf.

Val was self-conscious of her appearance and the effort it took and felt extremely vulnerable. She became irrationally irritated at Ryder for not being sensitive enough to her sudden emotions.

"Say something, jerk!" Val commanded while dragging her bag on its wheels through the airport as Ryder followed.

Ryder searched for words and felt bad he gave Val the wrong impression. Finally he said, "You look fabulous!" Ryder meant it sincerely, too. He wasn't just telling her what she wanted to hear.

They walked on as a smile subtly played upon her lips. Ryder kind of looked over at her reaction.

"Do you want a real laugh?" Ryder asked and Val nodded and he lifted up his baseball hat to reveal his self-inflicted buzz cut.

Val did not just laugh out loud, she guffawed so loudly heads turned from across the airport.

"I knew I could count on you not to make me feel worse." Ryder joked in a dead pan sort of delivery and then they both laughed together as they walked out of the airport and searched for John/Sven's borrowed car in the parking lot.

SOMEWHERE OVER THE PACIFIC OCEAN OCTOBER, 2019

While Val slept next to him in the airplane, Ryder continued to pour over his Uncle Williams notes and maps and input them into her phone. Upon his death, his Uncle William bequeathed them to his favorite, and only, nephew. It took Val quite a while to teach such a tech novice such as Ryder all the ins and outs of loading and down loading all of the coordinates and terrain changes and along with the latitude and longitude that they needed, but he was getting the hang of it all.

Ryder was amazed by it all. Thanks to modern technology, he was able to translate his Uncle William's knowledge from four decades ago into a step for step map that he and Val could now recreate on her cell phone, or 'magic' rectangle' as Ryder liked to call that device. They would be able to retrace every step that Ryder and her father and his Uncle William, and his friend Dave all took. Ryder could barely comprehend such a thing, he thought he would have to mostly go by memory, which was one of the reasons he never wanted to partake in this trip.

***

FLORIDA GULFCOAST
LATE JULY, 1982

Mrs. Nowacki generously asked Leanne if she would like to go to the airport with her to pick up and welcome her son back to America after that Tibetan ordeal. Leanne jumped at the chance but also dreaded it because of the tragic news she had to share with him. The problem was when to tell him. How to tell him about his would-be child was painful and yet simple in a way because there was no easy way so she would just say it. No creative lead-in sentence would dull the effect of the words that would follow. Leanne didn't know when she would get the opportunity to share such delicate and appalling news.

Ryder's mother was so excited that she talked incessantly to Leanne which made it easy for the young girl, this way she didn't have to make small talk. Her mind was focused on only one thing, getting Ryder alone and sharing with him the heartbreaking event that happened during his absence.

Her heart felt a jolt of heat when she saw him walking down the corridor from the plane with the usual jaunty bounce to his step. His hair was longer than she ever remembered, and a bit more wavy, and he looked relatively healthy considering the weight he had lost during his recovery.

Leanne demurely stood back and let Ryder hug his mother first. She was pulling on her fingers in nervous anticipation and it took all of her strength to hold back and let them hug. She wanted to run to him. As he embraced his mother she wept into his ear and he laughed and looked to tell her "I'm fine, I'm fine." Mrs. Nowacki was not pacified by his declaration and cried some more.

Ryder kept his eyes on Leanne as he continued to smile and let his mother hug him tightly.

Mrs. Nowacki eventually realized that her son also wanted to greet his girlfriend and so she said, "I'm sorry, honey, go see Leanne." Mrs. Nowacki squeezed her son's arm one last time and let him go.

Ryder walked a step and began to open his two arms and Leanne could not take it any longer and ran into the safety and love of his embrace. His arms provided a welcome refuge for her troubled soul. Leanne didn't cry, she sobbed, her whole body shaking, as Ryder continued to hold her tightly.

Mrs. Nowacki was touched by this display of love from Leanne to her son, though she didn't fully understand it. They had only been dating for what, maybe six or seven months? Could she really love her son that much that soon?

Ryder was also amazed by her unfiltered emotions of love and yearning for him. They had pined for each other in the past when they were apart briefly, but this was something deeper and more powerful.

Leanne finally gathered her wits about her and without lifting her head from his chest said through a very runny nose, "I'm silly, I'm sorry."

"No, no, I love it. I love how much you missed me."

"I did!"

"I love how much you love me."

"I do. For always and forever."

"For always and forever. You taught me that." Ryder backed her up a smidge so he could look at her face. She was self-conscious and embarrassed by what she assumed was a face messy with mucus and emotion. Her face was, but Ryder never thought it looked more engaging or resplendent.

When they got to their car, Mrs. Nowacki asked Ryder if he wanted to drive, "Since it's been a long time since you've been behind the wheel of a car."

"You can be our chauffeur!" Ryder suggested merrily and opened the back door for Leanne and him. He wanted to be as close as he could be to Leanne. He wanted their bodies to touch even if in a chaste way.

Mrs. Nowacki made a face but smiled eventually as the two teenage lovers sat in the backseat.

Leanne held Ryder's hand as they drove back home and her mind raced as to how to tell him what had happened in his absence. She had rehearsed so many different scenarios and ways to broach the subject but none of them were easy or smooth. She couldn't wait to be alone with Ryder, yet she also dreaded it.

Mrs. Nowacki took a left turn instead of a right turn to get to the Nowacki house and Ryder noticed it immediately. "Why a left turn, mom?"

"We have to drop Leanne off." Mrs. Nowacki answered casually, "Her mother said so when I called."

"Wait, what? Why?" Ryder asked with his voice rising.

"Oh no, please no Mrs. Nowacki!" Leanne pleaded as the tears welled in her eyes and soon poured down her cheeks. She didn't even bother to wipe them away. Leanne could not believe her mother would insist on her being taken straight home, but then the more she thought about it the more she believed it. Leanne felt her mother hated her and Ryder, really, she seemed to loath all love affairs. Leanne was desperate to speak to Ryder in person. She wanted to admit her sin, assuage her guilt, and hopefully have Ryder forgive and maybe even absolve her.

Mrs. Nowacki apologized profusely but said her hands were tied, she had to drop Leanne off at home.

"Can't you talk to her mother, mom, please?" Ryder beseeched his mother but to no avail.

"I can't, dear. You two can see each other tomorrow. What's another day after all this time, right?"

Ryder protectively put his arm around Leanne and held her tight for the last half mile to her house.

The two young sweethearts got out of the car once Mrs. Nowacki pulled into the Rhobbs' driveway. They stood off to the side and just held each other in a soul sharing embrace. As Leanne wept, Ryder whispered into her ear, "It'll be ok. I got you. I got you forever and for always."

Mrs. Rhobbs opened the garage door and nearly hit the two young lovers as they held each other tightly.

"Oh, hello Ryder, nice to have you back." Mrs. Rhobbs said dryly without an ounce of sincerity.

Ryder tried to let go of Leanne because her mother was there but Leanne would not let go of his arms.

"Thank you, Mrs. Rhobbs." Ryder said awkwardly as he both held and tried to unhold Mrs. Rhobbs' daughter.

"Ok, Leanne, time to go in." Mrs. Rhobbs commanded and then forced a smile to Mrs. Nowacki as Ryder's mother sat in the car and waited for her son.

"Mom!" Leanne yelled. "Just a little longer!"

"No, let's go, now." Mrs. Rhobbs said a little more stern and louder this time.

"Mom, no!" Leanne yelled again as her anger boiled over and mixed with her sadness and despair.

"It's ok, m'sweet. I'll see you tomorrow." Ryder reassuringly said in a soft tone while he gently squeezed her arms that were still around him.

Leanne looked at Ryder with love, and then over at her mother with anger, and then back to Ryder. "Promise?"

"You know I do, m'sweet. I love you." Ryder wanted to kiss Leanne goodbye but he didn't dare with Mrs. Rhobbs staring him down.

Leanne took it upon herself to reach up on her toes and kiss Ryder quickly, yet lovingly, on the mouth. She then whispered into his ear, "Call me tonight, I'll wait by the phone for your ring."

Ryder nodded to Leanne, and then sheepishly tried to smile at Mrs. Rhobbs who in turn looked away from the boy and grabbed her daughter's arm and led her forcefully back into the house.

Stunned by everything that had just happened between Leanne, her mother, and himself, Ryder walked, shell-shocked, back to the car and his mother drove him back home in mostly silence.

***

TIBET
NOVEMBER, 2019

As a trekking guide, Ryder loved watching the eyes of his clients as they took in once in a lifetime sights. Their joy and amazement turned into his and it made his job more than a job - it was actually a vocation - to share in their euphoria. This jubilation was doubled as he guided Val through the same steps her father took four decades previous.

Ryder never tired of hearing Val exclaim "Oh, ah!" almost every time they rounded a bend and caught a glimpse of the beautiful Tibetan countryside or people. Val was especially enamoured with the children of Tibet.

Upon seeing her cooing over a Tibetan baby on the roadside with her mother, Ryder smiled and said, "Look at you!"

"What?" Val asked as her finger continued to be held by the infant who looked up the American lovingly.

"Who would have thought you were such a softy?"

"That's our secret. I'm a tough chick, don't ever forget it!"

The nice thing about travelling together isn't just all the talking and sharing that occurs, but also the silence. There are many hours and kilometers of riding or hiking in silence where you have time to think and your thoughts are not rushed or interrupted. There are no electronic impediments to deep contemplation. Their first week was just about over and they were excited to almost finally be out of the vehicles and onto their own two feet. They just had one more day until they reached Dojer's compound where Ryder, Val's father, and his Uncle William and friend Dave all stayed.

As Val travelled deeper into the Tibetan countryside her initial thoughts were about her father and what his reactions might have been to the wondrous topography that unfurled itself so dramatically. She wondered if he was as wide-eyed as she was about it all. She told herself he probably was.

While Ryder and Val rode in a boxy, small truck from the early 1990s and bounced violently this way and that on a bumpy and lump dusty road, her mind then meandered where it often did in quiet times, and that was to past disastrous choices and regrets. Val tried not to let her thoughts sit in this dark and ugly room too long though.

"What a day!" Val said brightly to Ryder, but more to herself, to shake off the dust and dirt of shame.

Ryder sensed this and after an appropriate time of silence, he asked her, "Did you ever get close to getting married?"

"Did you?" Val shot back.

"I asked you first!" Ryder retorted and slightly laughed.

"No, not really. I could imagine all sorts of men I could fall in love with, I just never met them."

Her words hung there in the truck as every jolt and thump sent the two passengers east, west, north and south simultaneously.

"What about you? Why isn't there a Mrs. Nowacki?"

"There was."

"There was?" Val asked in astonishment, she thought she was informed he was single all of his life.

"Yes. My Mom was Mrs. Nowacki." Ryder laughed at his own joke but Val did not. She just scowled playfully at him.

They resumed looking out of the window the best they could with the rough condition of the road.

For his part, Ryder was trying to ascertain if he really remembered these places and features or if he just thought he did. He had Val's phone with the coordinates plotted out so he knew through his Uncle Williams detailed notes that he was following precisely the path that he did back in 1982. Strangely, it mostly seemed new to Ryder. Although he was sure nothing changed much in those forty years everything looked fresh to him. Or maybe it was Ryder that changed mightily since 1982.

Yes, Ryder acknowledged, that was most certainly what it was.

***

FLORIDA SUNCOAST
JULY, 1982

Ryder rang Leanne's phone later that night and she picked it up before the ring was even in its first full second of sound.

"I'm so happy you called!" Leanne whispered excitedly as she cradled the phone receiver near her ear and laid on her bed. "I couldn't wait another second and thought I'd explode and then, RING, there you are!"

Ryder laughed and then seriously told her, "I love you so much, Leanne. I'm so sorry about today."

"My mom is the worst!"

The two young lovers rehashed the drama of the earlier encounter and exchanged more platitudes of love, devotion, and yearning to be together. All the while, though, Leanne was troubled.

Ryder noticed her mood and asked her about it and her eyes welled up and she began to sniffle but couldn't speak. "What's wrong, m'sweet, what do you have to tell me?" After asking her this question Ryder pictured something terrible that she could tell him, like she fell in love with someone else, or had an affair in the couple of months he was away. His mind then thought of - "

"I did the most terrible thing!" Leanne finally said and now Ryder's stomach was really turned into knots.

"What did you do?" Ryder asked with more tension in his voice he had hoped to let escape.

Leanne rehashed their romantic last night together and then how she felt sick and tired for the next month or so and then mentioned how her sister Jolene had a friend that had a sister..but Ryder wasn't following her train of thought. "Ryder, I was late, like , very late and I took a test and, I was."

"You were what?" Ryder asked, wondering if he just wasn't hearing all the words she was saying.

"I was pregnant."

"You're pregnant?" Ryder asked loudly and in a panic.

"No, no, I was but I am not now." Leanne assured him.

"Oh." Ryder said, feeling relieved. But then it hit him, "But, how? How were you pregnant but aren't now."

Leanne told him.

As every detail was explained his tears now joined hers. "No Leanne, no!" Ryder implored.

"I didn't hear from you! I didn't know what to do!" Leanne said, trying to defend herself to both him and herself.

"I know, m'sweet, I do, but that was our baby. Our baby!" Ryder saying those words made it all too real for the both of them and they both just sobbed on the phone to each other. Finally, tragically, Ryder said the words he would forever regret, "I just don't know how you could have killed our baby without even talking to me about it."

Leanne was not sure she heard him correctly and asked him to repeat himself. He did not.

Ryder instead said, "I mean, I love you so much and I would have loved our baby so much if you didn't -" the words stopped but they ended too late.

Leanne hung up the phone and then buried her face in her pillow and tried to scream, cry, and punch her pain away.

Ryder was left speechless. He knew he went too far and was too harsh, but he also did not expect Leanne to hang up on him in the middle of all that. He also knew he couldn't dare call back because her mother would pick up and yell at them or worse, pick up and listen to their conversation. The Rhobbs only had two phone lines in their house and either could be picked up almost anywhere.

As sad as Ryder was, he honestly was also angry. He wasn't sure if he was angry just at the circumstances, or if he was also angry at Leanne. The first instinct of any father should be to protect his children and that was what came to the forefront of Ryder's emotions upon hearing that devastating news.

Ryder paced around his room trying to clear his head and think. He had to be quiet as it was late at night and he didn't want to have to explain anything about this to his mother if she were to wake up.

Ryder thought about sneaking out his mom's car and driving over to Leanne's house and getting the ladder from the back of her house and climbing up to her window to apologize but he wasn't sure she would open it for him. Plus, if her parents found him there, or if a neighbor drove by again and called the police…

Ryder said her name outloud, softly, "Leanne Rhobbs." Ryder said it a couple of more times and then thought of a Bruce Springsteen song called "Thunder Road" and how it sounded like her name. He always loved that song. He had it on a cassette tape, taped off the radio a year ago for free.

He grabbed a notebook and played the song, line by line, and changed the words from Bruce's to his. He would write a love song and apology song using the melody from "Thunder Road" and then give it to Leanne. He began writing, listening, writing. He finally finished just after 2 am.

Some of the lines were forced, or corny, but many of them spoke volumes of truth to his love and devotion to Leanne, and his hope for a reconciliation. Where Bruce sang, "Well I'm no hero, that's understood, all the redemption I can offer girl is beneath this dirty hood" Ryder instead wrote, "Well I know your parents hate me, that's understood, because I need danger and adventure and run around like Robin Hood".

Ryder also touched upon their energetic and innumerable bouts of pre-marital bliss, where Bruce sang, "they scream your name at night in the streets, your graduation gown lies in rags at their feet" Ryder instead penned, "You scream my name as we lay on your sheets, our times alone together are such tasty treats".

Ryder then put his 'song' into an envelope, addressed it to Leanne Rhobbs, put a stamp on it, and then snuck outside and put it into the mail box with the flag up so it would be ready to go out the next morning. Ryder figured it would take a day, maybe two to get to Leanne. In the meantime he'd hope and wait for her to call him but he wouldn't call her for fear of her parents getting angry or her getting upset all over again with him.

Ryder made sure he was going to be busy the next day so he wouldn't dwell or perseverate on Leanne and their fight. He also didn't want to think about what she did to their baby back when he was injured in Tibet. It crushed him to think that they could have had a baby together and now they won't. He called Billy and they arranged to go along with Billy's father out on the Gulf in their boat for off shore fishing.

The next two days were a blur of activity but the one thing Ryder did not do was answer a phone call from Leanne as none were forthcoming. Nor for a third day, or fourth day either. Ryder was now frantic. He wondered if his letter with the altered worded song actually made it through the mail to her house.

The letter did. Mrs. Hobbs saw it on the second day, when she got the mail and brought it in. She took it to her bedroom and then into her bathroom where she locked the door and then opened it and read it. She was aghast. There were references to her daughter and Ryder making love, him sneaking into their house and her bedroom in the middle of the night, and their plans to get married once they graduated high school.

The letter then waited in her night stand drawer under various papers and books until her husband came home from work at which point he read it and was also aghast, and angry at his daughter but especially at Ryder. He knew he could trust neither, but Ryder least of all. The boy was ruining his daughter's life.

Ryder tried to call Leanne after the four days went by without any contact from her. It was a risky thing to attempt but he was desperate to speak to her, to explain, and most of all just to hear her sweet voice. There was no answer for the first six rings and then a weird recording came on saying to leave your name and number. The Rhobbs had bought an answering machine so they could now screen the calls coming in. They altered the ringer so the phone could not be heard ringing but a light would go on the answering machine if a message was left. Ryder knew better than to leave a message.

Ryder did the only other safe thing he could think of, he wrote Leanne another letter. This was just a letter, not a song, and it explained in detail why he was sorry and what he was sorry for. "I don't regret a single time we made love, but I am so sorry to have gotten you pregnant and then weren't here to help you make your decision. I miss you and love you and can't wait to marry you and then we can have all the babies we want, no matter what your parents say!"

These words, and all the words Ryder wrote, were read by Mr. and Mrs. Rhobbs and never by Leanne. The words Ryder wrote in those two letters were then read the next week by the school board of the Catholic high school that both Ryder and Leanne attended, after the Rhobb's parents called a special session. Mr. Rhobbs being a board member made convening this meeting easier.

Everything was happening way too fast for Ryder. Yet it was the unknown that was eating away at his sanity. Why hadn't Leanne called him back after his song and letter? What was she thinking about him? Did she still love him? Why hadn't anyone answered the Rhobbs phone for the past week? And what happened to his Uncle William and his friend Dave? The last anyone heard they were both still in a hospital hopefully recovering on the other side of the world.

A week later Ryder got the notice in the mail from his high school that he was expelled on the grounds of 'moral turpitude'. Mr. Rhobbs, a skilled attorney, was moving quickly as a shark would if it smelled blood in the water. Only in this case, it was Mr. Rhobbs that was dispensing the blood, and all of it from Ryder's veins. His mother handed Ryder the letter and demanded answers. The day after that another notice came, this one with the authority and crest of the country seal on it, informing him he was not to go within one hundred yards of the Rhobbs house or Leanne. His mother demanded answers from her son about that. When Mrs. Nowacki wasn't satisfied with her son's explanations, she put in a call to the Rhobbs parents and dutifully left a very pointed message on their newly installed answering machine.

Mrs. Nowacki got a phone call back from an irate Mr. Rhobbs an hour later who angrily filled her in on all the details, all of them. Every last salacious detail. Mr. Rhobbs had made copies of her son's love letters and wanted to know if she would like a copy for her own perusal. He also mentioned to Mrs. Nowacki that he had a police report in his possession that detailed a potential burglary attempt at his house in the middle of the night. Leanne's father explained that a neighbor had spotted a ladder leaning against the Rhobbs house at just after 4 am and the policeman responding to the call identified the suspect as a 'sixteen year old male named Ryder Nowacki', though at the time no charges were filed.

When Mrs. Nowacki tried to stammer a reply Mr. Rhobbs cooly informed her that unless she kept her son away from his daughter he would pursue charges against Ryder and that he planned on prosecuting to the full letter of the law. Mrs. Rhobbs stood near her husband and smiled at him proudly and was impressed by his ruthless efficiency and calculated detachment as he dismantled a sixteen year old boy's aspirations. As a couple they didn't always see eye to eye but on this matter they were in lock step.

Life as Ryder Nowacki knew it had crumbled and ended. At sixteen years old he felt he had come to the end of himself.

***

TIBET
NOVEMBER, 2019

Dorje's compound finally and joyfully came into view and it couldn't have come at a better time. Neither Ryder nor Val felt they could take one more jarring bump in that truck from the pot hole filled road. They were both eager to get to the trekking and hiking part of this trip where they only had their legs to propel them and no longer would be at the mercy of uncomfortable trucks and roads that were barely there, barely roads at all. They felt stodgy and wanted to work their muscles.

As he got out of the truck and looked around, first stretching his back this way and that, Ryder thought the compound generally looked the same but he also knew his memory from that many decades ago could not be fully trusted. He bent down into the back seat of the truck and took out his rucksack and got a thick manilla envelope out of it. He then looked through the contents of the envelope while Val loosened up her stiff legs and their driver unloaded the bags from the top of the truck.

Ryder held up a five by eight photograph and looked at it, then looked at the compound, then back to the picture.

"What's that?" Val asked, noticing what her travel companion was doing. She walked over to see.

"My Uncle William had taken so many photographs with his big, expensive camera when we were here way back. I'm just comparing this compound to when we were here last and if it changed much. I didn't think it did but, looking more closely, I guess my old brain was wrong. Look there." Ryder said pointing first at the picture and then at a building that had sprouted up since he was there last. "That one is new."

Val noticed it and nodded.

"By the looks of the windows, size, and ventilation, that must be the new dry toilet building."

"Dry toilet?"

"No flushing water for, ah, you know, and no running water for hand washing." Ryder explained, "It's too small for anything else."

"What did you do way back in 1982, to, you know, before this was built?" Val asked but in some ways didn't really want to know.

"There was a very small, wooden structure with a bit of a plasticy thing with a hole in the middle of it and two wooden planks for your feet as you stood over it."

Val spouted, "Bletch!" Ryder whole heartedly agreed with her assessment.

"It took a lot of getting used to. Hopefully this -"

"Gsang Bchol." A short, very old man with a flowing muti-colored robe - called a chuba - and flowing white hair walked up from behind and said to them. He also wore a belt, a hat, and boots.

"You aren't, " Ryder asked, studying the man, "you aren't," Ryder sifted through the photographs until he found the one he was looking for. "Dorje? Is this you?" Ryder showed the older man a picture.

"That was me. This is me now. Which do you like better?" Dorje asked first Ryder and then Val, with a bright smile.

The two men hugged. "It's been a while, even for Tibet." Ryder commented while Val looked on.

Dorje looked over to her and raised his eyebrow, Ryder understood. "Oh, she's my friend Valerie."

Dorje bowed and said "Namaste."

"Namasete." Val said back to the older gentleman. "And what were those two words you said to us when you walked up?"

"Gsang Bchol." Dorje said and then paused. He had a regal way of speaking. As if he was a wise man down from the mountains. "It means depository of secrets."

Val took a beat to understand exactly what he said and what it meant, and then laughed loudly.

"That's about the best term I ever heard for one of those things!" Ryder said and then Dorje led them into the large building near where they were parked but he first stopped and held out his large, weathered hand.

Ryder was confused and just stared at the old Tibetan man. "Twenty yuan this time!" Dorje said and then laughed so loudly birds flew off a building many meters away. "Last time it was only five yuan. But at least you get to sleep indoors this time, no tents!"

Ryder was amazed that Dorje remembered so vividly not only the sleeping arrangements they had back in 1982 when they visited for one night, but also the price they paid.

Ryder paid him happily and then Dorje walked them around and showed them how little and how much things had changed in those many years. They encountered several people. Dorje explained to Ryder and Val who they were to him, their names, and their age. The number of relatives that now lived there on Dorje's compound was impressive. Dorje was proud, as his relatives were too, of how many years they were on Earth. He kept repeating his age, 88, and the ages of whichever relative he was introducing, with pride.

"It's not like that in America where we come from." Ryder stated, "Everybody hides their age and tries to surgically make themselves look younger."

"Odd." Dorje commented.

Ryder nodded, "And sad."

Dorje showed them to their room. It was a simple affair with two cots and a nice window that overlooked the courtyard, and the imposing, majestic and very beautiful snow capped mountain range that loomed behind it.

"Rest, dinner is in a little time. Someone will rouse you when it is ready for you to join us." Dorje said and then bowed, left their room and closed the colorful and heavy wooden door behind him.

Val sat on her cot as Ryder put his rucksack onto his. "I kind of don't want to just rest, really."

"No?" Ryder asked as he started to look through his rucksack for a fresh shirt to wear for dinner.

"No. Let's take a little walk, get a bit of a stretch of the legs and see those crazy gorgeous mountains!"

"Really? Ok. Sounds actually like a great idea." Ryder agreed and stood up, unzipped his rucksack shut so no creepy crawlies would find their way into it, and outside into the evening air they went.

They walked briefly to the edge of the clearing, before the fields where highland barley, also known as Qingke, was growing in an ocean of black and purple that swayed in the constant breeze that came down from the mountains. Dorje preferred growing this because it was able to flourish in the cold and was drought-resistant. He got top price for this crop at the market as it was used to make Tsampa, which was a roasted barley flour, and a staple food in the Tibetan diet. Some even used the barley to make barley wine, which Dorje also did and was planning on serving it at tonight's feast for his two American guests.

Ryder and Val stood shoulder to shoulder, not talking, just gazing up at the vast and towering jagged white peaks in front of them. They were silent and awe struck. Had it not been a slightly cloudy day they might have been able to see the outline of Minya Konka off in the distance to the east. Finally Val softly said, "Thank you."

Ryder understood and simply replied, "My pleasure."

Val then hooked her arm around Ryder's shoulder and gave it a squeeze. Their height difference made this less than a smooth move. "Thank you." Ryder said and waited for her to ask.

"Thank you for what?" Val inquired.

"For the most awkward semi-hug I think I ever experienced." Ryder laughed and Val pulled away and then hit him in the shoulder.

"You ruin everything!"

"You wouldn't like me if I wasn't me!" Ryder said amidst another laugh. He wasn't sure if it was the altitude or something else, but he felt giddy and young again. He was afraid he might be too playful and hurt Val's feelings and the rare show of vulnerability she displayed. He now turned to Val and hugged her with both of his arms going around her tightly and holding her still and apologized in a voice that was half sincere and half full of levity, "I'm sorry."

From a location hugged tight and deep into his chest Val's muffled response came out, "Big 'D' little 'ick'!"

Ryder let her go and looked at her in shock and asked, "Wait, what did you just say, or spell?"

Looking pleased with herself Val replied, "Big 'D' little 'ick'. That's what you were being, Ryder."

Ryder laughed loudly once it sunk in what she was saying/spelling. They wandered around the compound a little more until a young girl who looked to be about ten years old ran out to them and waved at them and tried to signal that it was time to gather in the main hall for the evening feast. The girl did this by motioning with her hand to her mouth like she was eating food and pointing to the larger building that was where the meals took place. Ryder and Val were charmed by her pantomime and gladly followed her as their stomachs were beginning to growl anyway.

The shutters on the many windows of the building were the same as Ryder had admired long ago, they were intricately carved and retained their colors of reds, golds, and blue. This sturdy structure wasn't going to erode or crumble in any millennium soon.

Inside were the same long wooden tables that Ryder and his uncle and two friends had eaten at long ago. Many women, of all ages, entered the building from the side rear door along with their army of children and grandchildren, and great grandchildren. Many men also entered the building but they came in from the massive wooden double front doors that also had intricate carvings on it. The men had been working in the fields and tending to the yaks, sheep, and goats.

After a few speeches and toasts by Dorje, everyone dug into their meals. Ryder ate mostly what he did when he was last there in 1982, and that was Dah Bhat. Due to Val's insistence, Ryder also tried some Momos filled with yak cheese as well as vegetable pakora. He liked them both very much. What he didn't enjoy was when he tried to wash it all down with Sea Buckthorn juice.

The face Ryder made when the juice hit his taste buds caused him to scrunch his mouth and cheeks in such a way that the children watching him laughed heartily at his discomfort. Ryder noticed this and took another swig of the juice and made the same faces just to hear the sweet sound of the children's guffawing.

During the entire trip so far Val had been on a mission to expand Ryder's palette and for him to at least try tasting more of the Tibetan foods. The foods he tried at Dorje's compound were added to a list that also included papadom, Tibetan bread, moringa, pickled daikon, and carrot pudding.

After she finished her meal, Val borrowed Ryder's envelope of pictures from the past and searched until she found the one of her father with the three year old Tibetan girl asleep peacefully on his lap.

"I want to meet her." Val said, showing the picture to Ryder. "I wonder how I can find her?"

"Dorje might know." Ryder said and walked over to him, showed him the picture and asked.

Dorje wasn't exactly sure so he asked his wife and showed her the picture. She was shorter, rounder, but just as vivacious as her husband, just maybe a decade or so younger. She nodded.

Dorje motioned for Val to follow him and they walked further down the table until they stopped next to a woman who sat with a sleeping baby in her arms. “This is her.” Dorje explained to Val.

Ryder walked over as Val was trying to communicate with the lady. Dorje interceded and explained in his native tongue of Tibetan, specifically the Khams dialect, what Val was trying to convey to her.

The woman pointed at the picture of the sleeping young girl, and then herself, and made a quizzical face.

Val nodded.

The woman now nodded and brought the picture closer to her face to examine it better. A smile now came to her lips.

“Her name is Tashi.” Dorje told Val about the woman she was talking to. “I told her your name as well.”

“Valerie.” Tashi said slowly in her heavy Tibetan accent. Val and Ryder both thought it sounded very melodic when Tashi said it.

Dorje said something more to her and she nodded again and smiled even brighter. Dorje said more to the lady, who was a second niece to him, and now the lady lost her smile. She looked up at Val and pointed to the man in the picture, Val’s father Nick, and asked in her native tongue if that was indeed her father. Dorje translated for Val and the American sadly nodded to the Tibetan woman who was roughly the same age as her. “That was my father, Nick. I heard that he loved playing with you and holding you while you slept.” Val explained to the woman through Dorje’s translation.

The woman thought about it, searched her memory for a flicker of recognition of Nick Brown, but there was none. Still, she looked at Val deeply in the eyes and stood up with the baby in her arms. The lady touched her own heart and then the picture of herself being held by Nick.

The lady then hugged Val with her free arm and Val hugged her back while also patting the baby. “Is this your baby?” Val asked her through Dorje’s translation.

Dorje answered for her, “No, this is her grandchild.”

“Grandchild? Aren’t you my age? Aren’t you only forty years old?” Val asked and looked at the woman with wonderment.

Dorje explained to his niece what Val said and the lady smiled, and then sweetly offered the baby for Val to hold. Val was touched by this gesture and carefully cradled the baby into her arms and sat down.

Ryder looked on warmly.

Val looked up at Ryder with eyes that bespoke both admiration as well as regret. “What am I doing with my life?” Val asked Ryder while keeping a soothing voice so as not to upset the baby.

“What do you mean?” Ryder asked.

“We’re both forty, her and I, give or take a few months I’m guessing. She has had children and now grandchildren. What do I have to show for these forty years? What’s my legacy? Who’s coming to my funeral?”

Ryder did not expect that stream of questions from Val but upon thinking about it, he came to the same conclusion. His life to this point was missing something. Maybe it was missing everything. What did he have to show for his fifty plus years? What was his legacy? Who was coming to his funeral?

“I feel the same way.” Ryder simply said as the same ashen look that was on Val’s face was now on Ryder’s.

***

FLORIDA SUNCOAST
SEPTEMBER, 1982

Billy had never seen his best friend Ryder cry in all the years they knew each other, but in the past week he'd seen him break down and sob on three occasions. This latest time was the most concerning. It was after two in the morning. Ryder had snuck over to Billy's bedroom window and lightly knocked and said his name until Billy finally woke up.

"Dude, what are you doing?" Billy asked as he stumbled towards the window which was open except for the screen.

"Billy." Ryder said frantically with a voice that was awash in tears. "I've got to see her! I tried to see her!"

Billy knew who the 'her' was, but he also knew about the restraining order and all the other legal roadblocks that Mr. Rhobbs had expertly set up. "Ryder, you can't see her. Wait, what, you tried to see her?"

"I love her. I love her." Ryder said in a trance-like voice as Billy fought through the fog of just waking up from a dead sleep.

"Wait, Ryder, did you try to see Leanne?"

"Yes, I love her and she loves me!"

"I know, I know, but you can't see her! Not now, not yet! Dude, what did you do?" Billy asked in terror at what the answer might be.

"I snuck into her house and made it up to her room, but the door was locked. I couldn't get in."

Billy could not believe his ears. "Dude, what?"

"So I knocked lightly at first, then louder, but she still didn't hear me. Then I hear her mother walk up and then yell 'who is that?' Then I hear her dad coming around the corner from his room and he starts to yell so I panicked and ran and jumped over the bannister all the way down to the first floor -"

"What?" Billy asked incredulously. "I can't believe you didn't get caught, or break your leg doing that!"

"I can't believe I didn't either! Then I ran out the front door and started running home but I thought I heard cop cars and sirens so I ducked out through the field and hid in the bushes and then ran here."

"So they're looking for you?"

"I'm guessing."

"They got a good look at you, her parents did?"

"Who else would it be, right?" Ryder asked, still sniffling. "I love her! She loves me! I can't just leave her!"

"Want to sneak in and hide here?"

"I don't know, I'm afraid this is the second place they'd look after my house. What do you think I should do?"

At that moment both boys heard sirens and the revving engines of police cars barreling down Billy's street. They had gone to Ryder's house and woken his mother up. Upon seeing there was no Ryder Nowacki in his own bed, they immediately deduced that he probably was at his best friend Billy's house.

"I have to go! If something bad happens to me - Tell her I love her!" Ryder ran off before Billy could even get another word out to his imperilled best friend.

***

TIBET
NOVEMBER, 2019

For the next few days on this arduous part of the trail neither Ryder nor Val talked as much as before. There were a myriad of reasons for Val, the utmost was her reflections on her life choices and where she possibly should have turned right instead of left or went up instead of down. The lady at Dorje's compound that her father held in his arms back in 1982 had really shaken her. Val had a car, a credit card with a high limit, fancy indoor plumbing, and yet she felt the Tibetan woman was much richer, and much happier. Val felt like Tashi was a much more fulfilled woman with a clear sense of purpose.

Also, Val loved Tashi's style in clothes.

Val loved them so much she bought many garments from one of the women in the compound and now wore them everyday of their trek. It was a colorful and comfortable ensemble. It kept her much more cool in the heat of the hiking day but also much warmer as the shadows crept in during the evening hours.

Val, though, when she was being brutally honest with herself, knew there had to be many more changes ahead for her in her life.

Ryder wasn't as gabby the last few days since leaving the compound either. He also doubted many of his choices over the past four decades. Was so much of the violence and anger he was a part of really necessary? Ryder wondered if the self-imposed emotional exile of the past several decades was also the right decision. When he was being brutally honest with himself he knew he was wrong in so many instances and possible courses of action. Ryder shrugged his shoulders as he scrambled up a boulder to get to the next flat section near a stream and asked himself silently, "But what can I actually do about it all now?"

The terrain was getting more difficult and the climbing was progressing to a more technical level but physically they were both excelling. A lot of the trail and its wonders Ryder recollected and would sometimes tell Val anecdotes about either her father or his friends that happened at those places.

Val loved those moments especially. They made her feel at one with her father. She felt a thrill to be sharing his footsteps while Ryder shared his remembrances of her father's adventures.

As it was with Ryder back in 1982, in a long list of daily highlights, the bonfires at night were her favorite times. Fatigue helped make the food that Ryder prepared even more appreciated and sumptuous. The sleep Val experienced in the tent in her sleeping bag, packed tight against Ryder in his sleeping bag so they would be kept warm, came hard and heavy and rejuvenating.

The trekking continued on and the air got dryer and thinner and their throats were becoming raw and their muscles were feeling the effects of so many upward miles and meters. The days piled onto each other. Their spirits would flag and then a new spectacular vista would appear and then they would rouse themselves into a good mood again.

It always seemed when Ryder and Val were at their lowest that the greatest views happened.

This morning Val woke up with a headache that wouldn't leave or dissipate. Ryder had her drink more water than normal and gave her most of his ration. They stopped more often and he kept a sharp eye on her for any signs that she might be experiencing cerebral edema. Her energy was dipping as were her spirits. For the first time on the trip she thought about quitting. She thought maybe this was a stupid idea and they should just turn around and head back home.

"Ryder," Val said, but then hesitated. "I was thinking that maybe, I don't know, that maybe -"

"What's the matter, Val? Is it your headache? Is it worse?" Ryder asked with much concern and worry.

"No, it's not that, well, not just that. No, it's not worse, it might actually be going away a little. No, I just, I don't know, never mind." Val stopped herself. She didn't want to say the words 'I quit, I want to go back home'. She didn't even know which home she would want to go back to, the one in Cleveland or the new one she had been sharing with Ryder in Crested Butte, Colorado.

Ryder stopped her from going on. "Val, seriously, are you ok? What's wrong?" Ryder searched her eyes for an answer.

"Let's just keep going and then we can rest and maybe talk." Val said and started to hike forward.

They walked in silence, with Ryder looking over often but covertly, so she wouldn't know she was being watched. The path looked familiar to him, as if it must have been momentous all those years ago for some reason.

The trail turned a corner and then BOOM! There majestically before them, two miles away and nearly two miles up, was Minya Konka. It was the view that stopped the men in their tracks and his Uncle William then explained to them the meaning behind the word 'Darshan'. Ryder stopped and dropped his gear and told Val to do the same. He now took the time and taught Val the word 'Darshan' and explained the meaning to Val and that magical time with her father and friends back in 1982 when they all first saw the mountain.

***

"Who's the first girl you ever loved?" Val asked Ryder out of the blue. They had just boulder leaped across a frigid, shallow stream and came out on the other side to a lush garden of rhododendrons and Meconopsis. The white, pink, purple, and yellow of the rhododendrons mixed exquisitely with the vibrant blue flowers of the Meconopsis, also known as the Himalayan Blue Poppy.

Ryder did not look pleased to have heard this question and at first pretended he didn't hear Val ask it so he could just ignore it. "Careful on that scree, it can get a little slippery if you go too fast."

Val was not distracted by his ploy and persisted, "Ok, I'll be careful. So, who's the first girl you ever loved?"

Ryder gave Val a look that asked, 'Do we really have to talk about this?' But then he actually asked her, "Are you getting hungry?" Ryder thought this was a perfect way to change the subject because Val always badgered him to stop and eat and usually he would want to shoulder on a little further.

"Later." Val answered in a perfunctory way and got back to the business at hand. "Just answer!"

Ryder groaned and not because of the elevation of the hike that they were currently experiencing.

"Ok, fine." Val huffed and Ryder relaxed and was thankful that that question and answer session was over.

They hiked on for a moment or too in quiet peace.

Then Val asked, "Ok, who's the last girl you have ever loved?" Val smiled. "A ha! Different question!"

"Yes," Ryder sighed, "but it's the same answer."

***

FLORIDA SUNCOAST
SEPTEMBER, 1982

Ryder had always been a pretty fast runner all of this life. This came in handy during his baseball and football playing days. It was a nice luxury to have, to be able to beat out slow ground balls to the short stop or catch a football and quickly accelerate so a cornerback or safety doesn't plow into you. Speed on the playing fields was a liberating factor and often was the margin between victory and defeat.

Tonight, with Ryder running through the heavy, humid, insect filled air, it was also a liberating factor that was the difference between victory and defeat.

So far.

Ryder had sprinted away moments before the headlights of the incoming police cars illuminated Billy's driveway. The policemen then shined their spotlight into every window of Billy's house and the surrounding bushes. They summoned Billy and his parents and asked them if they knew about Ryder's whereabouts. His parents honestly did not. Billy answered that he did not know where Ryder currently was, which was technically true. They didn't ask him if they knew where he was just minutes ago!

Ryder had climbed up high in a tree just a stone's throw from Billy's house and watched the interrogation. He could hear sirens in the distance all around him and figured that was the safest place to be at the moment. He was proved correct.

Eventually the police left and the sirens' sounds dimmed and faded away. Ryder climbed down and pondered his options.

He knew he couldn't go home. Maybe not ever. That realization struck him like a gut punch.

He didn't want to go to jail but without any money in his pocket or transportation other than his quick legs he was stuck in that area.

Ryder then thought of the one place he wanted to be. He reasoned it might also be the one place the police would not be at anymore. He began his careful trek under the cloak of darkness.

To make it less scary and less real, he envisioned he was caught behind enemy lines in World War Two and the Nazis were after him. Him and his friends had done this countless times on the private golf course that bordered his neighborhood. The security detail of the golf course and its adjoining condominiums would chase Ryder and his friends throughout the bunkers and fairways and trails but never catch them.

Ryder knew the police would not be as inept as the private sector security guards, but what other hope did he have?

***

TIBET
NOVEMBER, 2019

Just as he had done all those years ago with his Uncle William, Nick, and Dave, when Ryder turned the corner and stepped out of the lush forest he saw the huge wall of mountains in front of him and the Monastery down low, almost as a tiny speck. Val was gobsmacked and just stopped, stood still, and soaked all of nature's majesty in.

"That never gets boring." Ryder quipped as he looked at Val and her astonishment that anything could be so imposing.

"We're not really climbing to the top of that, are we?" Val asked with wide eyes and a healthy dose of trepidation.

"No we are not. Not to the top anyway. But we are going up high. But look down there." Ryder said, pointing to the base of all of that granite grandeur. "See, at the bottom? That's where we're going next."

Val squinted and then finally saw it. "That's the Monastery?"

Ryder nodded and they began to walk towards it. Ryder had told Val just enough to whet her appetite for that place but didn't want to say too much about it in case the Guru was no longer there or it was deserted now. The Guru would be around 90 years old if he was still alive. Ryder didn't even have a hope the older lady helper would still be around, she would be over 100 if she was!

Three hours later they were walking into the courtyard of what looked to be an abandoned Monastery. The buildings were there, sure, and in decent condition, but there were no signs of life.

Suddenly Ryder perked up, "Hey! The tables and chairs are still there! Come on, let's go sit in them!"

Ryder jogged over to the sitting area and Val wondered why he did. It wasn't like there was anyone else clamoring to also sit in those chairs. "Such a little boy." Val said out loud to herself, with much affection, about Ryder.

"This is exactly where that one lady served up coconut wafers and lemonade! Right here!" Ryder exclaimed as he sat, beaming, in the chair. Val was bemused by his excitement and how his blue eyes seemed to dance.

"What are we going to do since no one is here anymore?" Val asked with a bit of nervousness.

"We can always pitch our tent here I guess. That's not what bothers me, though. I just really wanted you to meet the Guru, and walk around and see the inside of the buildings, and the colors, and that one room in the middle of the building - it was square and full of windows - where they would chant and play their instruments and read from their holy documents. Oh, it was an amazing experience! And the food! Oh my stars! The food!"

"Oh my stars?" Val repeated Ryder's expression and laughed. "What, are we back in the 1950s in Mayberry? Are you Aunt Bea?"

"I'm excited, so sue me!" Ryder retorted. "But talking to the Guru, oh man, did we all love talking to him! So calm and wise. I think I asked him about Leanne -" Ryder stopped himself in mid-sentence but Val heard him.

"Leanne? Who pray tell is Leanne? Who is this Leanne that she's so important you would ask the Guru questions about her?" Val asked, intrigued.

Ryder sat tight lipped and looked everywhere but at Val.

Val was not letting this go. "Who is Leanne, come on, tell me! We have nothing else to do in the vacated place! Oh wait, Leanne…is she the same answer to both questions? First love and last love?"

Ryder now looked at Val with a naked vulnerability.

Val met his stare and asked again, this time in a more softer manner, "First love and last love?"

Ryder stared at Val for a moment and then simply said, "Forever love."

***

FLORIDA SUNCOAST
SEPTEMBER, 1982

Ryder was correct, the police cars had left. He stealthily made his way closer to the Rhobbs driveway and once he got past the wall of bushes he could see their house clearly in the pale moonlight.

Ryder's heart tightened and his pulse raced as he saw Leanne's bedroom light was on! As he stepped closer he almost screamed in excitement and joy when he saw her silhouetted form walk into view.

He lost all pretense for stealth or unobtrusive movement and instead ran under her window. He could look up and see her standing there, pacing it seemed. He looked down and searched for a perfect size rock to throw up at the window to get his true love's attention. Ryder bent down and found one and reached back to throw it gently.

He was knocked to the ground roughly by an undercover policeman that was stationed on the Rhobbs family grounds. Ryder was almost rendered unconscious. He felt his left arm being forcefully wedged behind his back. He heard the clean metal jangling of the handcuffs and then felt them around his left wrist. He now knew.

"Leanne!" Ryder screamed with his face smashed against the hard concrete of the Rhobbs driveway.

The officer struggled to get Ryder's right arm and also wrestle it behind his back. "Leanne!"

Ryder just faintly heard a window above them open. He clearly heard a young female scream and then he heard his name. "Ryder! Oh Ryder!" He stopped squirming and the officer hand cuffed the teenage boy successfully.

"I love you Leanne!" Ryder shouted as the officer now stood him up. There was gravel stuck to his face and mixed in with his tears. Ryder looked up and saw Leanne leaning so far out of the window he was afraid she might fall out.

"I love you Ryder!" Leanne screamed in terror at the sight of him being led away by the police. Suddenly there was yelling coming from behind her. Her parents forcibly moved her away from the window and out of her room. She fought them but they were too strong and determined to not let her win.

"I love you Leanne!" Ryder yelled one more time as he was lowered into the back of the unmarked police car.

"Ryder! I love you! No, come back! No! I love you!" Leanne cried out one last time as the police car door shut. A high pitched wail of pain and sorrow bellowed from her open window as the car drove off into the night.

***

TIBET
NOVEMBER, 2019

Ryder thought he'd seen a ghost.

He couldn't speak and almost leapt from his chair when he saw her calmly walking up to them in the center of the square where they were sitting. It was her! She was still alive! "It's her!" Ryder whispered to Val who then nearly also leapt from her chair in fright as the sight of the woman came into view. It was the same grizzled helper to the Guru that Ryder and the three men had encountered four decades past!

Silent but dutiful, the woman placed down a tray of cookies and then returned back to where she came. Ryder and Val exchanged confused glances and then Ryder picked up a cookie and sniffed it.

"Well?" Val asked, feeling skittish about the whole thing.

"I don't know." Ryder replied and then put the cookie to his mouth and was about to take a bite when Val stopped him.

"No!"

"Why not?"

"It might be poison!"

"Why would some hundred year old woman poison us? She couldn't possibly even move our dead bodies away." Ryder said and then took a bite. Val waited anxiously for the result. "Coconut wafer!" Ryder exclaimed and then popped the rest of it into his mouth.

Val now reached for a cookie and took a bite as well.

The lady came back out with a pitcher of lemonade.

"Do you remember me?" Ryder asked, knowing full well she couldn't have. The lady said nothing, didn't even acknowledge his question or even his presence. "She's probably deaf by now." Ryder reasoned.

The lady walked back to where she came from and Ryder and Val ate and drank in astonished peace.

Within a minute of finishing eating all the cookies from the tray and emptying the contents of the lemonade pitcher the lady reappeared and motioned for them to follow her. When Ryder asked, using his hands, if he could help carry the plate and pitcher back she shook her head 'no', and Ryder was not going to argue with her no matter how much he wanted to be of assistance.

"It hasn't changed one iota!" Ryder marvelled as he entered the huge rectangular common room where he last ate dinner and talked with the Guru. The same rows of pillows lined the floor underneath the windows and the same bulbous pot belly wood stove gave off heat to warm the room and all those in it. The main pillow at the center of the room was empty, it was the Guru's place.

"Guru?" Ryder asked the centennial aged lady, hoping she would understand. He asked but was afraid the answer might be that the Guru is no more. If she understood what Ryder asked she didn't let on.

No matter, moments later the Guru himself walked through the same doors he had entered the room for the men back in 1982.

"Welcome!" The Guru said with a warm smile and a rather jaunty wave of his arm towards Ryder and Val.

"Thank you for your hospitality again, sir!" Ryder replied, genuinely pleased to see the man.

"Again?" The Guru asked and studied both Ryder and Val more closely, trying to remember them being guests in the past.

"Oh, so many years ago, sir. Way back in 1982. I was young then -"

"Weren't we all!" The Guru joked and all laughed, except for the helper lady who just went about her business of setting the table, arranging the pillows, and adding more firewood to the woodstove.

"True, true. I was here with three other men and we were on our way to Kora the mountain Minya -"

"Konka, yes, now I remember!" The Guru stated and Ryder wondered if he really did recall them. It had been so long ago that they were in his presence, and it was only for one evening and a short portion of the following morning. "Circumambulate is also known as Kora in my language, they are just a little different from each other."

"We had such an incredible time with you, such amazing hospitality and also knowledge that you imparted to us."

"That's all fine and good, but who is this beautiful young woman, your wife?" The Guru asked as he looked at Val and made her blush.

"Oh, no, I'm sorry, where are my manners? This is Valerie Brown, she is the daughter of one of the men I came here with at that time."

"Valerie Brown, it is my pleasure to meet you and have you here in my gurukul here at our monastery."

Valerie shook the Guru's hand and shyly smiled and replied, "Oh, thank you so much, sir. I really appreciate you letting us visit."

The helper lady finally spoke, but only to the Guru and only in their native tongue. "Time to eat, I hope you both are hungry."

They were and it was a delightful and sumptuous feast. Ryder, thanks to Val's cajoling, added another new food to his growing list. This one was called Bhagsta Markhu and once Ryder tasted it, he loved it and then devoured a second helping. It was a kind of Tibetan sweet mac and cheese.

"See, you should listen to me every now and then for a change!" Val said to Ryder as she watched him finish that treat.

"Yes, you should always listen and heed your girlfriend, Ryder." The Guru said as he watched them both interact.

"No, she's not my girlfriend, she's my friend who is a girl." Ryder tried to explain but the Guru wasn't so sure and showed this doubt through his facial expression. "No, really, she's, she's the daughter of Nick Brown that visited you with me."

"That may be true but it is also two very different things that do not cancel each other out." The Guru calmly said.

The Guru had a soothing way of speaking that made you sit on the front of your chair and lean in to listen.

"How is your father, Valerie?" The Guru asked and Ryder felt a protective wave overtake him for Val.

"Oh, sir, her father -"

"It's alright, Ryder, it's ok. I've made peace with it." Val said reassuringly to Ryder. "After that visit to your monastery way back then, my father was killed in an avalanche on that mountain."

The Guru reached out and put his hand over Val's. "And you were very, very young weren't you, Valerie."

Val nodded but tears did not start to well up in her eyes. She just looked at the Guru and felt peace.

"You were so young you probably don't remember much about your father except for the fact that he loved you very much." The Guru continued as Valerie listened attentively. "That love will never leave your heart nor your soul."

Valerie felt so comforted by the Guru's words, and his tone of speaking, that a wave of tranquility like she'd never known washed over her. All she could do to show her gratitude was to say to the Guru, "Thank you for that, sir."

The Guru smiled and then motioned for them to move away from the table and over to the part of the common room where all of the pillows were laid out. The Guru sat in his usual spot and Ryder and Val each sat off to his right, near the wooden stove. The dry heart emanating brought even more solace.

"Do you have children, Valerie?" the Guru asked.

Valerie hesitated but then truthfully answered, "No, no children. I never got married either. I guess it's too late."

"No, it's not too late." The Guru surmised.

"Well, it's not too late to get married but it is to have children now. I'm forty with no husband or even a boyfriend and none in sight!" Valerie explained and tried to keep her tone light though the realization of her words and situation did make her feel a certain darkness. Her mind flashed back to Tashi, the lady from Dorje's compound who her father in that photograph had held decades previously, and how she had a fulfillment and joy that Valerie could not picture ever having.

"You have time. You needn't feel stressed over this. Good things are on the way to you, Valerie." The way the Guru said it made Valerie begin to believe it.

The Guru now faced Ryder and spoke, "You are older than Valerie, but you seem to be close to her soul age, are you not?"

Ryder had never heard that expression, "I really don't know, I don't know what a soul age is to be honest." Ryder paused thinking the Guru would explain but instead the older man just looked at the two of them sitting there. "I guess we seem pretty equal in energy levels and our way of thinking about things, and situations. I guess we are pretty close in soul age, even if I am an old man compared to her!" Ryder said with a laugh and hoped the other two would laugh as well since he felt a little uncomfortable with this line of discussion. The Guru did not laugh, but he did smile at Ryder.

"This is why you two travel well." The Guru stated and both Ryder and Val thought about it and had to agree that might be one reason. "Ryder, you have unfinished business on that mountain."

Ryder pondered what the Guru meant by that and decided that he did. "Yes, I never really looked at it that way, but I reckon I do." Ryder expected Val to laugh because every time he would say the word 'reckon' Val would make fun of that expression and say he sounded like an old-time cowboy, but this time she did not.

"You do. You left the mountain on bad terms last time. This time you must find peace there."

"I will try." Ryder replied simply.

"Have you any children?" The Guru asked him and Ryder shook his head 'no'. "A child's innocence is a reminder of the purity and goodness that exists in the world."

"I love children, I think. I haven't really been around any in a long time but they seem sweet and fun."

"If you have children and they have children and then it's like you live forever. Children are the living messages we send to a time we will not see."

The Guru let those words sink in and all was quiet in the common room except for the occasional crackling of the firewood as it burned in the wood stove or the tinkling of cups and dishes that the helper lady was putting away.

The Guru sensed what Ryder and Valerie might be thinking and answered them, "I have taken a vow of celibacy so I will never know the pleasure of having my own children. But there are many male children that train here and study Buddhist philosophy, logic, debate, and other subjects. They are my living messages that I send out to a time that I will never see. And it brings me peace."

"That sounds wonderful." Valerie said sincerely.

"It is. Children are wonderful. Also wonderful is giving of yourself. Like your Jesus always talks about, caring for others. Don't think less of yourself, think less about yourself. Happiness often comes when you are not always thinking of yourself, and instead are doing for others and loving your neighbor even when they might not seem to deserve it and you might not want to." The Guru said.

"Kind of like our ten commandments?" Ryder said.

"Precisely. Only ours are called the Ten Courses of Wholesome Karma. A person who follows these can develop mindfulness and compassion. They are also keys in productive parenting."

Ryder and Valerie sat there and absorbed the Guru's teachings but also wondered why he was singing the benefits so eagerly of parenting when neither of them had children nor any prospects for them. The Guru watched their eyes that betrayed their inner thoughts and then he added, "Good things are coming to you both. Just remember as you go forward, eat half, walk double, laugh triple, and love without measure." The Guru then closed his eyes with a contented smile.

Neither Ryder nor Valerie knew if they should say something, or just sit quietly until he opened his eyes again, or maybe just carefully stand up and leave the room. They exchanged unsure glances.

With his eyes still closed the Guru then spoke and asked, "So what is it you hope for, Valerie?"

"On this trip or in life?" Valerie asked.

"You tell me whichever you feel comfortable with."

"I don't know, really. On this trip, I hope, I , I really don't know what I hope to get out of it." Val said.

"Hope in my culture and sphere is controversial. Some preach that hope is something we need to give up, ye tang che, which means totally completely exhausted or as you Americans might say, totally fed up. It describes complete hopelessness. This is an important point. Some think that is the beginning of the beginning, completely giving up hope."

"Wait," Valerie interjected, trying to sound as respectful as possible, "giving up hope is the beginning of the beginning?" Ryder was also skeptical of what the Guru just said but kept it to himself.

"Yes. It is thought that without giving up hope -a hope that there's somewhere better to be, that there's someone better to be - we will never relax with where we are or who we are. We could say the word mindfulness is pointing to being one with our experience, not disassociating, but being right where we are right at that moment. Does that now make better sense to you both?"

Ryder and Valerie both answered, "Yes." They were riveted by the Guru's words and explanations.

"To think that we can finally get it all together is unrealistic. To seek some lasting security is futile. To undo our very ancient and very stuck habitual patterns of mind requires that we begin to turn around some of our most basic assumptions. Continuing to seek pleasure and avoid pain, thinking that someone out there is to blame for your pain, one has to get totally fed up with this way of thinking. One has to give up hope that this way of thinking will bring satisfaction. Suffering begins to dissolve when we can question the belief or hope that there's anywhere to hide."

Ryder and Valerie both sat, listened, and nodded. The Guru spoke slowly in a way that kept the two Americans hungry for more of his words, ideas, and teachings. They were a captivated audience.

"Hope and fear is a feeling with two sides. As long as there's one there is always the other. Hope and fear come from a feeling that we lack something, they come from a sense of poverty. We hold on to hope and hope robs us of the present moment. We feel that someone else knows what's going on, but that there's something missing in us, and therefore something is lacking in us. This is where renunciation enters the picture - renunciation of the hope that our experience could be different, renunciation that we could be better. And then there's the renouncing of liquor, or sex, and so on and not because those things are inherently bad or immoral, but that we use them as babysitters. We use them as a way to get comfort and distract ourselves or escape. The real thing that we renounce is the tenacious hope that we could be saved from being who we are. Renunciation is a teaching to inspire us to investigate what's happening every time we grab something because we can't stand to face what's coming. Do you see?"

Again both Ryder and Val silently nodded and waited eagerly for more of the wise man's words.

"On the other hand, some think hope is a less focused word for positive intention. That it matters what your positive intentions are. That we should be encouraged to practice the Noble Eightfold Path and hope can be found in every practice. Trusting in the immeasurable value of the Three Jewels. Being steadfast in virtue, in encouraging the positive potential of other beings. All worthy goals, yes?"

"Yes." Ryder and Val answered.

"Some teach we should give up our desires and attachments. You may ask, does that mean giving up my career, my mortgage for my house, giving up music and other pleasures, my spouse, my children, and other desires? How is it possible to have no desires when all we do require some element of desire? I do not believe so personally. I do not believe we should end desire and attachment. I do believe we should end the clinging and craving to self as an actual existent thing that endures and persists over time. I believe living for me, me, me, is a recipe for loneliness and unhappiness. I believe if I help someone finish a race that was stumbling it is far more noble and noteworthy than if I finished the race in first place. The greatest reward is the one I help you win, especially if nobody knows I helped."

The helper lady then came in with a kettle of masala tea and a plate full of Khapseys and the night's lessons were over. Ryder and Valerie said their thank yous and goodbyes to the Guru and made their way to their room. Bucolic sleep came easy for Ryder and Valerie with a peaceful contentment that often accompanied arduous physical activity, delicious food and consequential truths.

For the next few days of trekking the Guru's words were never far from their minds in their more quiet moments on the trail. As the hike climbed higher and higher through the thinning air they both had to stop and rest more often and that was usually the only time they could speak.

The paradox was that the Guru's message was basically 'think of others more and yourself less' and yet since they left the monastery they had almost exclusively thought of themselves and their life journeys so far. It was almost as though they had to purge their self-directed thoughts through this marathon session of introspection before they could then free themselves to focus outwardly.

It worked.

As Ryder approached the magic area he had longed to see again since 1982, he had spent any last realms of narcissism. Val had also cleansed herself of any of the remnants to an egocentric world view. They both wanted to devote themselves to something bigger, to someone else other than themselves.

"I've been so eager for this moment! I'm so excited to bring you here!" Ryder said as they approached a wall of rocks that at first looked like it had no access for entry. But going a few meters closer, Ryder was able to point out the slender opening. Ryder waved Val over and then he disappeared into the granite opening. Upon entering, he looked at Val and saw that the place had the same magical effect it did on her as it did on his uncle and two friends those decades past.

The rock threshold led to a gorge that opened up to the secret valley the four men enjoyed so long ago. Ryder and Val might very well have been the only people since then to have found and enjoyed that spot.

Val was amazed at the expanse of undulating grassland that went for a couple of miles and the giant cliffs of their mountain that rose sheer and forbidding in true Tibetan style. She had never imagined such an Eden-like paradise could exist. Val thanked God that she could be so blessed to partake and enjoy this secret valley's bountiful riches. She then thanked God for Ryder coming into her life and making all of this come to fruition.

Ryder for his part let her stand there and soak it all in. Her joy was his joy and that simple fact made him happy and led him to believe that maybe he was changing for the better and becoming less selfish and more selfless. He readied camp and when she offered to help he insisted that she just wander around and explore the wonders and just be in the moment. He set up the tent, collected the firewood, and then had a roaring fire burning within the hour while Val did as she was told and immersed herself in this breathtaking and clandestine concealed Tibetan treasure.

Ryder then explained to Val how his Uncle William had taught them men about polar plunges and how they first tried it out in the stream down the ravine. He suggested that she do it too and she agreed.

As she took off her many layers of clothing Ryder tried not to watch her undress but he found his eyes constantly returning to her ever more naked form. When she got down to her barest coverings he turned away and began to pound the stakes to the tent into the ground. She walked over and stood in front of him wearing only a towel and asked, "So just a little bit down the hill and there's the stream?"

Ryder smiled and nodded and tried to not look like he was ogling her though he knew he was.

When she got back and was full of goosebumps but also refreshed from the polar plunge, Val both looked around and marvelled at her surroundings while also looking at Ryder and marveling at what an impressive man he was. He was a flurry of activity in their camp site just so she could enjoy herself and treasure this moment. Val wasn't surprised by this, though, he often was doing much for her, and at what benefit to himself? What did he get out of all this kindness to her? She was moved at how she thought about him putting his life on hold just so she could achieve this dream to visit the mountain that claimed her father.

Maybe that was it, Val wondered. Maybe Ryder felt an indebtedness to her father and was repaying that through guiding her. Either way, it was a touching gesture from a man she had grown very close to. She wondered if he felt the same way about her or was she just a burden to him? Was she just a duty he had to fulfill? As the food cooked on the bonfire and he finally sat down she decided to ask him directly.

"Ryder, why?"

"Val, why what?" Ryder asked in return with a half smirk.

"Why are you so kind and doing all this for me?"

"You are very easy to love." Ryder did not mean to say that sentence. He didn't know how he had said that sentence. What he meant to say was 'forget about it, it's no big deal' or something along those lines. He didn't add to the sentence or say anything to subtract from it. Ryder just let the words sit there at the bonfire with them, surrounded by all the imposing beauty and grandeur of Tibet.

One moment had been running through his memory during many silent times during their trek. He had been at work, maybe a month ago, when he walked past one of the grocery store windows and peered out. There he saw Val. She must have borrowed one of his bikes from the Krammitt Inn and rode into town. It wasn't just the way the sun shone in her hair or the alluring form that her bike pants and low cut top accentuated. It was the fact that she was talking to this older homeless man. Talking to him and listening to him.

Ryder thought that man is probably rarely ever really seen or heard, and here was Val taking the time and effort to do both. That touched Ryder and made him see Val in a much fuller and deeper way. She took her time and patiently didn't rush him when the older man spoke. Ryder noticed and was moved when Val lowered her head to fully hear what the man was trying to tell her.

When she then walked with the man and bought him an ice cream cone, and made a point to have multi-colored sprinkles decorate the top of it, Ryder first felt he was falling in love with her.

Val's mind was racing as to the meaning and purpose of Ryder's words. He had never said anything even close to that in all the time she had known him. He never even seemed to be that emotionally deep or interested in a relationship or in anything like that whole romantic world. Val wondered where that sentence came from and what it meant. Val also wondered when he was going to speak and hopefully clarify everything. She dreaded being the one to ask him, she didn't want to come across as needy. The silence finally got to her and she felt like she had to ask.

"I'm very easy to love?" Val finally asked, timidly, hoping if she used his own words it wouldn't make her seem demanding or clingy, two things she swore she would never be. She prided herself on being independent and strong. She now wondered if that was a wrong assessment of herself.

Ryder took his time answering but this time didn't feel like hiding his true self, his true new self actually. "You are very easy to love. You really are. There's so much about you that I've discovered I love about you." Ryder spoke soulfully and slowly, almost as if he was in a daze and Val momentarily thought maybe he was experiencing altitude sickness and his brain was cloudy.

The other thing that Val thought was that she felt excited that this might be true, his love for her. She didn't know it was something she wanted until this exact moment. But now that it was here it seemed so natural and so right.

Val had not recalled ever being this scared as she was at the instant, because nothing before ever was this important to her. "So you're saying…" Val asked Ryder, letting the silence linger until he decided what he really wanted.

Ryder turned to her on the stump they were seated on and looked directly and deeply into her guardedly optimistic eyes and stated, "I'm saying I love you. I've fallen in love with you Valerie."

Valerie stared at him and waited for him to either say something more or do something. Then it dawned on her, he was being respectful and most likely hesitant himself to do anything more until he knew her feelings. She felt thrilled, and suddenly free. She threw her arms around his neck and hugged him tightly and laughed out loud.

She then backed her face up to examine his, he was beaming right back at her. Valerie then closed her eyes and moved in closer and they kissed. And then deeper and longer and more passionately. Valerie felt like she had never kissed anyone before it was so new and overwhelmingly otherworldly. And soon dinner was forgotten and the bonfire was left to tend to itself in that secret valley of bliss and consecrated dreams.

***

FLORIDA SUNCOAST
SEPTEMBER, 2019

Ryder had been sitting in the holding cell for over eight hours now. The wooden bench was hard and the bars on the walls were cold but he was trying to be thankful that at least he was there alone. Then he heard a slow walking sound of professional shoes on the concrete floor. He wondered if it was a guard bringing him elsewhere, or maybe letting him go because he posted bail.

It was neither.

Mr. Rhobbs strode into the area of Ryder's holding cell with a sinister coolness about him. He stopped in front of Ryder's cell and took out a piece of paper from inside his sport coat breast pocket. He then carefully took a fancy pen from the other pocket in his sport coat. "You can sign this or you can stay in jail for a very, very long time."

"What is this, Mr. Rhobbs?" Ryder asked cautiously but respectfully.

"Read it. By all means read it. And then if you're smart you'll sign it. And then I never want to see you again. Ever." Mr. Rhobbs said with just a trace of anger rising in his voice and his eyes locked onto Ryder's.

"Can I have my lawyer look at it first, Mr. Rhobbs?" Ryder asked after reading the first few sentences.

"This is between you and me. This is your only chance to avoid serious time. Do you want to be incarcerated?"

"No, of course not, Mr. Rhobbs, it's just that -"

"Then don't sign it. Either way I will get rid of you."

Ryder read the rest of it and his will melted away. He signed the sheet of paper that Mr. Rhobbs forced upon him and his hope drained away. He was going to be going across the country to finish high school and live with his Uncle William in Colorado. He would agree to never contact Leanne by phone, mail, or in person. He would, in effect, make himself invisible and disappear from her life. Or he would spend considerable time in a real jail. Mr. Rhobbs gave him the choice of a quick death or a slow one.

There were already two signatures on the document. One was Mr. Rhobb's signature. The other was Ryder's mother's.

***

TIBET
NOVEMBER, 2019

There was one last push to reach the lower walls of the north-west ridge, the same location of the deadly avalanche from when Ryder was there last. There was snow everywhere on the ground and in the air. The wind gusts blew it sideways into their eyes. It was the opposite of the conditions when he was there with Val's father, his Uncle William, and Dave. And Ryder was very thankful for the colder conditions.

There was a much less chance of an avalanche on this day, so far anyway. Ryder kept a sharp eye for any signs of something that might be treacherous or ominous. Val had been a trouper the whole climb and especially now. She listened to whatever directions Ryder gave and never whined or complained about the conditions.

There was no talk between them of what happened back in that secluded paradise in their tent, at least not yet, though it was constantly on both of their minds. Each wondered what the other was thinking but was too timid, or afraid of the answer, to actually ask. Val especially thought that maybe she had made a mistake in thinking that Ryder was sincere. She wondered if she should have kept her heart guarded. The silence between them regarding that ardent evening was tortuous for Val.

Her fears were unfounded, though.

Ryder felt himself falling in love with her even more with every passing day and now he was almost paranoid in his efforts to keep her safe and free from harm. This was no easy task on this dangerous mountain.

They made their way across the ridge a little farther and briefly rested and Ryder debated about telling Val that this was where her father died. He ran through the pro and con arguments through his mind and then decided that she could take the truth. That's why she came here after all, to see and experience it all. "Right down there, " Ryder said, pointing to the spot that he remembered like it was yesterday, "that's where I last saw your father alive. And then it all happened."

Val's eyes scanned the area that Ryder spoke of, and then looked above it at the wall of snow and ice. He could see the trepidation in her eyes.

"That's why we're not going to stay right here too long. Maybe a moment more or two, ok?"

"Ok." Val said softly and took it all in. 'So this is where it all happened', she thought as she took some pictures with her phone, but then with the temperatures being below zero her phone started to seize up.

"This way." Ryder shouted to be heard over the gusting wind and he led her safely away from the most dangerous area. "How are you doing?" Ryder tenderly asked her.

"My lungs and legs feel ok." Val answered without really answering what he wanted to know.

"How about your heart?"

"I'm sad. But I'm ok. Really."

Ryder then took the time to point out where various events that tragic day had happened, and the time line they occurred in. He pointed to where his uncle was on the ridge, where Dave got knocked down and Ryder went to assist him. He then reluctantly showed Val where her father was struck down.

Ryder paused and gave her time to process and soak in all the information he just imparted to her.

"Let's put our gear down here for a moment, I want to show you something. If you're sure you want to see it."

"Yes, I want to see everything. I want to see it all. I can take it." Val promised.

"If you're sure."

"I am." Val stated, and hoped she really was.

"Ok, this way." Ryder instructed and led her up and over a ravine and past some boulders till they got to a set of fathomless crevasse near the edge of a rather deep precipice. "But be careful!"

"I will be!" Val pledged.

As they gingerly stepped and dug into the snow upward and sideways, Ryder suddenly stopped and just stared.

"What? What do you see?" Val asked, intrigued.

"It can't be!"

"What?"

"I'm not sure. Wait, wait here, don't move!" Ryder stressed. "Don't move a step. It can be slippery. Promise!"

"I promise." Val said and stood still like a statue.

As Ryder got closer and closer to this one crevasse he started to think the altitude or the blowing snow was playing tricks on his eyes, or mind. The colors were identical to the colors that…it couldn't be!" Ryder kept moving closer and dreading that what he thought it might be actually was - it couldn't be! But upon closer examination, it indeed was. The colors he saw were the colors from the scarf that Nick Brown was wearing the awful day he was killed. And the scarf was still wrapped around Nick Brown's neck!

Ryder felt like he was looking at a ghost! He didn't know if he should go back and tell Val or just pretend he didn't really see anything and it was just tricks being played with light and snow.

He had to tell her, he owed her that.

As Ryder carefully made his way back to her non-moving place he wondered how he could soften the blow of telling her what he saw. He was too tired to think of anything creative, he was feeling weak and fatigued from the climb and the thin air, so he just blurted it out when he got to her.

"Val, I saw him."

Val couldn't hear him clearly and thought he was congratulating her on not moving, "Yep, I stayed still! Just like you told me to! So, what was it you saw?"

Ryder motioned for her to sit down and he sat down next to her. It felt good to rest and catch his breath. "Val," Ryder painfully started, not really knowing what to say or how to say it, "I saw him."

"Him?"

"Your father."

Ryder couldn't quite see the look of shock in disbelief in her face behind her sunglasses and mask, but it was there.

"My father? But how? You told me you and your Uncle William buried him in a sleeping bag and lowered him into a deep crevasse."

"We did, Val, I swear we did. But these crevasse's are always moving, it's like they're alive, and I guess with all the churning and freezing and unfreezing it must have worked your father back up to the surface. Some of the ice can get sharp as knives and it probably ripped open the sleeping bag. I recognized the colors from his scarf."

"His scarf?" Val asked and then reached back into her bag and unzipped a side pocket and took out a bag that was fastened closed. "You mean this one?" Val asked and lifted the small piece of her scarf that they had sent to her mother years ago. She gave it to her daughter who now brought it on the mountain.

"Yes." Ryder replied solemnly.

"I have to see him." Val said, starting to stand up on slightly wobbly and fatigued legs from all the hiking.

"Are you sure? It's really quite unreal! It's like, it's like it was yesterday. He looks like, your father looks just the same as he did way back when." Ryder explained hoping to caution Val on what she was about to possibly witness.

"I have to." Val declared and grabbed onto Ryder's sleeve and he led her carefully past the other crevasses while the wind continued its relentless blowing.

As she got closer she could see the colors that first caught Ryder's eyes when he walked up. The colors stood out brightly amidst all that white snow. And then she saw the full billowing scarf dancing above a lifeless human form, her deceased father. Ryder held her with both arms now as she moved closer on her unsteady legs in the gusts of snow.

Then she was there, standing right next to her father. Nick Brown looked mostly like he had just lay down for a wintry nap and hadn't woken up yet. The crevasse and the sub zero temperatures had perfectly preserved him. His dark, wavy hair was tousled and yet still full. His skin was pale with a blueish tinge but all in all he still very much retained the look of Nick Brown. Except for some pictures Val had never gotten a good look at her father and now she was seeing him as he looked on his last day alive, 37 years later.

The shock of it all hit her instantly and she almost could not take it. The trek, the physical exhaustion, the thin air at that high altitude, her possible future with Ryder, and now seeing her father this close and in this pristine condition caused her to start to black out. Ryder caught her before she fell. He laid her gently in the snow and hooked up an oxygen tank he kept for an emergency and applied it to her mouth.

Her breathing was good and he checked her pulse and then her pupils. Val began to return to him. "I'm sorry."

"Stop it!" Ryder said back to her lovingly. "You have nothing to be sorry for. Are you feeling better?"

"I'm sorry." Val repeated. "I'm usually not such a drama queen."

"I'll forgive you this time, but next time -" Ryder was going to joke about heaving her off the mountain but then stopped himself as he thought that might be too macabre.

Val now stood and looked at her father again. "He sure was handsome." Ryder stood next to her for both physical as well as emotional support.

"He sure was." Ryder agreed.

Val leaned down and tenderly whispered to her father, "I love you, Daddy." Ryder saw some tears start to trickle down from daughter to father. Val then put her hand over where his heart was under his heavy down jacket. "I love you."

Ryder put his arm around Val and held on to her as she looked at her father and wanted to memorize every detail of his face and form. She then looked at Ryder and he could see her frozen tears chilled to her cheeks. "Can you help me bury him again?"

"You mean back into the crevasse?" Ryder asked and Val nodded. "Of course I will, my love." Ryder then began to move Nick's body but then stopped and just stared at him too. Ryder now felt tears rolling down and freezing on his cheeks. Nick Brown was a kind and fun friend to him. Ryder loved him and missed him. This hurt him too. Ryder, in a way, felt like he was also saying goodbye to his younger self, when a world of opportunities still lay ahead of him. When Ryder still had hope for so many things. But what did the Guru say about hope? Ryder knew his grief couldn't come close to matching Val's but he was still filled with sorrow. And falling in love with Val and seeing her suffer intensified the downhearted emotions.

They went to work at the task at hand and did their best in order to honor Nick Brown and his wonderful legacy of love. Gravity helped the two immensely and soon he was interned back into Minya Konka for posterity.

The two silently bowed their heads. Their prayers were silently given to God while they huddled close together for emotional sustenance as well as warmth.

Ryder did not want to rush Val but he also knew the sooner they started to go down the mountain and breathe in the air from below the better. Val did not argue nor show any more emotion about the burial or the decision to leave and soon they were losing altitude and gaining oxygen.

As they continued to descend, Ryder would occasionally pat her softly on the arm and she appreciated the gesture. He would also intermittently ask her, "Are you doing ok, darling?" The way he called her 'darling' made Valerie feel strong and surprisingly summery inside her soul.

By evening they had picked out a campsite where the temperatures felt much warmer than zero and there was no danger of an avalanche.

Ryder again offered to pitch the tents and start a fire but there wasn't enough firewood handy this time so instead he had to make it with their portable liquid fuel stove. "You can get our sleeping bags ready though if you want." Ryder asked and Valerie dutifully complied and went into the tent and began to do her assigned chore. It didn't take her long and soon she was out of the tent and looking around at the scenery. The mountain itself was an imposing sheer wall of white but the sky was darkening exquisitely with a combination shade of blue and orange. One last huge soaring bird circled overhead before nightfall took over and it had to return to its nest.

When Val finally turned around and looked at Ryder he was kneeling down on one knee next to the small fire the portable liquid stove gave off. "What are you doing? Isn't the stove working? It looks like the fire is going."

Ryder then held up his hands, cupped together, holding a gold carabiner in lieu of an engagement ring, and asked Val, "Will you marry me?"

Val at first was going to laugh at his joke but then realized he was serious. She stared at him in silence, almost not being able to let the moment sink in. It had been quite an emotional day.

Ryder spoke again, "When I prayed by your dad, by my friend Nick, I asked him for permission, for your hand in marriage. My heart tells me he gave me that permission to ask you. Valerie Brown, will you marry me?"

"Yes, my love." Valerie answered from Minya Konka.

***

NAPLES, FLORIDA
AUGUST, 2020

When Dave got the phone call he immediately went onto his computer, logged into his trading account and bought some high yield, long maturing government bonds. He was sitting outside in his Florida backyard and had to choose between putting down his drink or his cigar to facilitate the trade, he chose his cigar.

Dave then went into the house that he paid cash for and found the box of stationary his mother had bought for him many years and decisions ago.

The nap he took earlier that afternoon helped him feel lucid, sober, and ready to write a letter. On the way out of the guest room with the box of stationary in hand, Dave passed a mirror and noticed that he was smiling.

Dave returned back outside and stopped and looked out on the intercoastal waterway that bordered his backyard and marvelled at the beauty of his surroundings. He gazed out at the water and the way the evening sun danced on the rippling waves. He loved watching the tropical birds that dove into the water and danced in the sky. Dave walked out onto his dock and sat back down in his chair. This was his happy place. He just thought he'd be happier if he was sharing this magnificent view with another person.

The letter was quickly written. He was brought up right and did things like this. If he checked out of a hotel he always left a twenty dollar bill on the dresser. If he got a great table at an exclusive restaurant he always rewarded the martie d' with a 'paper handshake'. Dave gave his mail man a bottle of scotch every Christmas, unless of course she was his mail woman and then he gave her a bottle of Chardonnay. And when one got news like he just got, he bought a government bond that matured in twenty years and wrote a letter.

He hoped his sons would do the same some day.

***

WAKEFIELD, MASSACHEUSTETTS
AUGUST, 2020

Leanne Tortelli, formerly Leanne Rhobbs, poured herself a second glass of Malbec and glanced at her watch and was disappointed to notice that it wasn't yet five o'clock. She shrugged her shoulders and chalked it up to a warm summer's day that deserved to have wine sipped in the sunshine, though she knew better.

Leanne hadn't meant to look in that box in the storage room. It had sat on that shelf for more than a decade. But she needed to find her immunization records and thought that that box might be where they were. They weren't. But the picture of her and Ryder at his junior prom were.

There they both were. Smiling sincerely, not a wrinkle or crows feet in sight, tight and lean everywhere, gloriously happy and unencumbered by the weight of the world or worn down by the lies of the insecure and duplicitous.

There in the photograph in her hand that did not hold the wine glass was the proof that her eyes could not deny even if her memory tried to, she was once thoroughly and daily full of joy.

Sure, now she found happiness in her two sons and comfort in their house and the new car that her husband leased for her every two years. Many days she had several moments of happiness, but not long lasting joy.

After both of her parents died they carelessly left behind many papers, documents, and even journal entries. Each folder was another revelation to the deceit that they perpetrated not only on her, and Ryder, but also on themselves and their marriage. Past shady indiscretions and dark deeds now saw the light. Leanne finally was able to read the letters Ryder had penned in another lifetime ago. She also read the threats, both legal and otherwise, her parents inflicted on the poor boy.

Through misting eyes the same sentence sliced throughout her soul and left bloody lacerations, 'if only I knew then what I know now.'

As she had done many times before, she started to write a letter but only got as far as, "I found a picture of you" and then put down the pen.

Leanne knew there was no use.

She lost any hope but unlike the Guru had explained to Ryder and Valerie, Leanne's hopelessness was not the beginning of a beginning but instead the beginning of the end.

Hearing her sons playing soccer in the backyard and knowing her husband was not home from work yet, Leanne snuck into the garage and quietly laid the now empty wine bottle into the recycling blue bin underneath some old cardboard pieces so there would be no evidence.

***

CRESTED BUTTE, COLORADO
AUGUST, 2020

Mr. Kravitz took a tissue from the tissue box on the side table next to his comfy reclining chair in front of his picture window and cleaned the lenses of his binoculars. There had been no movement around his neighbor Ryder Nowacki's house for over a day but the impotent voyeur wanted to be ready just in case. He looked at his watch and noticed that his wife had been away for another extra long afternoon of strenuous errands. Mr. Kravitz was thankful she enjoyed her weekend gallivanting throughout the town, at least that way he did not have to. He was thankful for the peace.

As a car entered his neighbor's driveway across the street, Mr. Kravitz hurriedly shoved the tissue into his shirt pocket and lifted the binoculars to his eager eyes. Mr. Kravitz sat up taller in his chair and tried not to blink.

An exotic lady with long flowing hair and a colorful long flowing dress stepped out of his neighbor's kitchen and waited next to the driveway along with a huge Bernese Mountain dog that stood next to her, energetically wagging its tail. After all these years Ryder Nowacki was no longer just a one dog guy, he adopted a new one.

A car that Mr. Kravitz had spied there before parked and then an enormous man got out, followed by his neighbor Ryder and then that slightly younger and shapely woman who appeared to be holding…

John/Sven, Ryder's best man, who had helped drive them to the hospital now brought them back home in his car. Mesa, Val's maid of honor, had stayed back to take care of their dog, Buster, and to get the house ready for the new arrival of Ryder's and Valerie's latest and greatest adventure together.

Nick Darshan Nowacki was born the day before, August 29th, 2020, and was 7 pounds and 1 ounce.

The beginning of the beginning had begun.

THE END

www.ingramcontent.com/pod-product-compliance
Lightning Source LLC
Chambersburg PA
CBHW070616310726
48982CB00001B/101

9798990936751